PRESTO

PRESTO

or
The adventures of a turnspit dog

written and illustrated by

MARILYNNE K. ROACH

Houghton Mifflin Company   Boston   1979

Library of Congress Cataloging in Publication Data

Roach, Marilynne K.
  Presto: or, The adventures of a turnspit dog.

  SUMMARY: A young dog escapes the drudgery of an
inn's turnspit to become a part of the colorful street life of
18th-century London.
  [1. Dogs–Fiction. 2. London–Fiction] I. Title.
PZ7.R528Pr   [Fic]   79-11746

ISBN 0-395-28269-1

CONTENTS

To W. S. Lewis

PRESTO

CHAPTER I

*Wherein our hero's captivity is lightened
by the beginnings of hope.*

There was once a small, grimy terrier who viewed his world
through the whirling spokes of a turnspit wheel, which was
wheel and cage in one. Its spokes were also bars, and the whole
was suspended at its axis with the dog inside, so that the floor
moved under his paws if he took a step. No matter how long
he ran, he remained in one place, with the full glare of the fire
heating one side of him and the cold draft from a door chilling
the other.

Except for the briefest recollection of his puppyhood, his life
had been passed in the wheel, which moved a belt, which in
turn drove other wheels that turned a spit of roasting meat. The
inn where this creaking prison operated, Fortune's Whim, was
famous for its roasts. The dog knew them only by scent.

1

During off-hours, when he was chained in a corner of the yard with a plate of meager scraps, he could just see the painted inn sign swinging over the front door. It showed the Wheel of Fortune, with happy ragged people rising up one side while surprised prosperous types tumbled down the other.

In contrast, the little dog proceeded nowhere. At first he almost accepted this, once his fear of the noisy contraption faded, but he began noticing little by little that this was not the only possible fate in the world.

There were two other animals living at the inn. The resident mouser, Nimrod, a big golden cat, came occasionally to sit by the hearth and talk with the dog. There was no cage for him.

And recently Mrs. Otway, the landlady, had acquired a lapdog with nearly as many pretensions as she herself had. His mother had been a French papillon of the type whose long silken hairs had graced many a parlor cushion. His father had been a small, rough-coated terrier. The landlady named him Fuzz. No one put him in a wheel.

There was no name for the turnspit dog. The humans called him "mutt," "cur," and "stupid," if they referred to him at all.

Then the stranger came.

*

It happened on one of the Twelve Days of Christmas, when Fortune's Whim was usually most busy. In early afternoon of this day, however, there was a lull when the kitchen staff was out, so the upper chambermaid felt free to let in a stray human and feed him.

The stray was a hungry young man, and Dog noticed that, after he cast a longing eye at the roasting mutton, he took time to look kindly at the unhappy creature turning it. They regarded each other through the spokes for a moment until the chambermaid fluttered over and propelled the young man to a seat. She produced some cold leftovers from lunch, and his attention was wholly taken up with them for some time.

The dog plodded on.

Nimrod materialized at one side and settled down compactly. "He's been here before."

"What?"

"When you were in the yard once. He's different from the others."

Dog kept an eye on the people, cautiously, since he could not turn his head far lest the spokes catch at his nose. The chambermaid was draped over the back of the man's chair, but his attention never really wavered from the plate until he had wiped it clean with a piece of bread and eaten the bread.

"She addressed him as 'Dick Oakes' the other day. I gather he's an entertainer of some sort."

Today she was calling him "Dicky," which he evidently disliked, and, although he had no hackles to raise, he did frown when she said it and got red about the ears when she persisted.

As for entertainment, Dog knew only what he heard from the cat or overheard from the humans. The stranger *was* different from the others, though. As Dog ran in the wheel, it occurred to him that this Dick had acknowledged the animals' presence without a display of annoyance.

"Look at her," said Nimrod. "The hypocritical miss."

She was fussing with Dick's collar and trying to examine his jacket lining, twittering on about their ragged state. Dog had never before seen her show concern for another. Dick plainly doubted her sincerity now. He stood up and went over to the hearth to warm his hands, thus missing the shadow that hulked past the window toward the stables. The chambermaid did see it, and sat down crossly.

"Was that the hostler?" asked Dog.

"Yes," said Nimrod, who had a clearer view. "So that's her game."

"I don't understand."

"She wants to make him jealous with the stray actor, of course. Won't *that* be a sight."

Dog was not so amused. The hostler's rages were well known at the Fortune, and Dick was a much smaller man in all directions. He was, furthermore, standing by the wheel and looking right at Dog as if he was sorry for him.

"Ho, presto," said Dick softly. "How fast the little dog runs."

The chambermaid, assuming he had spoken to her, resumed a cheerful expression and came over. But when Dick asked her the dog's name, the smile slipped a bit and she shrugged, saying, "That's only the turnspit."

Dick seemed annoyed by her remark but continued to watch the dog in the wheel. "Presto," he said. "I believe 'Presto' would do for a name."

Dog nearly lost the rhythm of his steps in his surprise, so it was just as well the humans' attention was caught by a sharply yapped command at the inner door.

Fuzz had come down from the landlady's private parlor for something to eat.

The chambermaid took the occasion to declare that if Dick liked dogs, this was a *real* dog. She began addressing Fuzz in

4

a sort of baby-talk and looked as if she would have liked to pick him up. But Fuzz was inclined to nip and disinclined to take impudence from servants.

He glared at Dick. "Who's this?" he barked. "You know Mrs. Otway doesn't allow strays here."

The maid, still cooing, set a bowl of bread and milk before him. He sniffed it and consented to eat.

"Presto," said the turnspit dog. "A name. I like it and it fits. Nimrod," said Presto, turning to the cat, "he gave me a name."

"Well, well. I never saw you show so much spirit before."

"But a name. I never knew . . ." He continued to mull over the idea, which seemed more and more fitting as he considered it.

The maid, meanwhile, was questioning Dick about his trade, and found, to her annoyance, that he was not a stage actor at all. He was a puppeteer. He warmed to the subject of his act while her interest flagged visibly. She kept glancing toward the window that overlooked the stable yard.

Fuzz finished his meal, licking the last drops from his muzzle. He swaggered over to the fire, keeping his distance from Nimrod, however, and stared at Presto.

"What was it that stray called you? Pesty?"

"It was Presto. Get it right."

Nimrod raised an eyebrow in surprise.

Fuzz bristled in astonishment. "Oh, indeed. How very continental."

"What do you mean?" Presto snapped, turning his head as far as he dared. Fuzz tended to prance about as he talked.

"It's Italian," said the cat. "*Presto* means 'quickly.' "

"My mother was French," Fuzz was saying, "but you don't

5

see me putting on airs with foreign names. A certain appropriateness of style . . ."

"They ought to have named you 'Bottle Brush,' then."

"Bravo, Presto," said Nimrod. "You *have* changed."

Fuzz gargled with rage and danced from foot to foot. "Impudence! Don't you know your place?"

"Whatever my true place is," shouted Presto, "it's not here in this machine!"

"Stop that barking," said the maid. She rattled a wooden spoon on the spokes of the wheel and then scooped up Fuzz, whose own barks had turned to coughing. "Did the nasty little cur yap at our Fuzzy? Go back to your nice parlor, where you won't be bothered." She went out with him still snarling and struggling in her arms.

But Dick was grinning at the turnspit dog. Presto grinned back, something else he had never done before. Already Dick had taken on an individuality the dog could recognize. While he knew the different people who worked at the inn, they were just humans to him, different members of one unpleasant pack.

This Dick was a lean young man with kind eyes and sandy hair that tended to escape from the queue he wore in it. Presto sniffed and memorized the man's scent.

The maid returned, and they could hear Fuzz barking somewhere else in the building, the noise hardly reduced at all by intervening doors.

Dick stood up to look around for his muffler and hat while the maid tried to persuade him to stay a bit longer.

Nimrod stirred and stretched his considerable length. "He puts up with her only for the food."

But now, perhaps because of shame or perhaps because he

6

had just eaten, Dick seemed about to show resolution. The
maid fussed over winding his muffler. Then — Presto was
watching his eyes and saw when he decided to bluff — Dick
made to repay the chambermaid in her own coin.

He grasped her suddenly about the waist, lifting her off balance, and placed a noisy kiss in the center of her astonished
face.

Nimrod swiveled his ears toward the sound.

Then all the doors seemed to burst open at once, and the
kitchen filled with people.

"Well," said the landlady, who had come in with Fuzz jumping at her heels.

" 'Ere now," growled the hostler, looming behind Dick.

Presto lost his stride and tumbled around in the wheel a few
turns until he could right himself. There seemed to be more
people than ever pressing into the room, all talking at once.
Nimrod flattened his ears in annoyance at the din and slipped
away from Presto's range of vision to his customary lair behind
the cupboards.

The chambermaid was in the corner, pretending to weep
loudly, while the hostler grasped Dick by the muffler the girl
had so carefully arranged for him moments before. Fortunately
for him, Mr. and Mrs. Otway spun him around by the shoulders to demand just what he was doing, thus disengaging the
hostler from his person. The hostler now held only one ravel-
ing end of the muffler, but continued to shout questions until
the landlady rapped him sharply with a spoon lying at hand
and bade him hold his tongue.

Presto gnawed at the wooden bars in agitation.

The cook, whose special domain the kitchen was, shouted

7

from the doorway while the kitchen staff twittered behind her, all crowding for a look. The landlord's young nephew, with whom the inn had been plagued for the holidays, squeezed into the room on hands and knees between the kitchen maids' petticoats and began hopping about, shouting, "Fight! Fight!"

With him pranced Fuzz, yapping continually. He danced over to Presto and leered. "I *told* you, mistress doesn't allow beggars."

"You told her," Presto exclaimed, and hurled himself at the bars, only to find himself tangled in the bottom of the swaying wheel, much to Fuzz's delight.

Although Dick had been talking nonstop, none of the other humans in the room was accepting his excuses. The hostler seemed ready to disassemble his supposed rival, and the landlord spoke loudly of the constables, somehow having gotten it into his head that there had been a burglary attempt.

Dick looked really desperate, when the cook shouted, "I smell burning!"

Everyone turned toward the fire, where the joint of mutton was quietly smoldering, for when Presto had stopped running, the spit had stopped turning.

There was a rush for the meat, and Presto began running, but the damage was done. The cook kicked the cage and he fell.

In all the confusion, not even Presto saw Dick slip out the back way.

CHAPTER II

*In which further human confusion provides
opportunity for canine freedom.*

Fortune's Whim did a bustling trade during the Twelve Days
of Christmas, and it seemed the spit was hardly ever empty.
Presto — for he had taken the name to himself completely —
plodded on longer than ever, until the last roast was ready to
serve and he was taken from the hot hearth to the cold yard.
He huddled his aching body in an overturned barrel, curled
tight in the meager straw, and snatched brief sleep until the
round of labor began again.

Yet his former blank endurance was replaced with the
thought that beyond the inn were people like Dick. The
thought proved such a torment that he actually snapped at the
odd-jobs boy, who was shutting him into the wheel. This
earned him a cuff on the head, but no blow now could shake
loose the idea of liberty.

On another occasion the wheel was still so that the cook's assistants could lift out one roast — juicy and done to a turn — and replace it with a spit of raw meat. Presto found himself idly chewing on one of the wooden spokes with the sudden realization that he often engaged in that nervous habit. Moreover, he recollected seeing tooth marks on the wheel when he had first been forced into it.

Suddenly, he could imagine a series of wretched little dogs running madly through time to cook a long succession of roasted meats upon which fell a pack of humans who devoured them with much snarling and cuffing down to the last scrap of gristle.

Nimrod regarded him differently these days. "You never used to show such spirit," he said, glancing at the odd-jobs boy, who was binding a not very clean rag around his wounded finger.

"I must get *out!*"

"Stop that dog's noise," the cook shouted.

The boy pounded the wheel with the satisfaction of approved revenge, and laughed when Presto lost his footing and rattled around for a few turns.

He was up and running with the agility of much practice, yet he despised himself for jumping so quickly to their bidding.

He stopped.

The wheel swayed a little and the spit remained motionless. Presto felt a little thrilling sensation he thought sure must be liberty, but the cook noticed the absence of the machine's rattle before he could savor it. She shouted again, and the odd-

10

jobs boy with a look of real pleasure jabbed a piece of kindling through the spokes at the dog's ribs.

Presto dodged it with only partial success, but his sudden moving of the wheel pushed the spokes around against the stick, which promptly snapped. Half plopped into a pudding set nearby, and the rest of it shied off the boy's head.

Nimrod chose to disappear in the ensuing turmoil.

Although Presto was soundly cuffed for his defiance, it was discovered that one of the spokes had split and wanted mending before the machine could be used. So Presto at least had the satisfaction of a rest in the yard while the odd-jobs boy was obliged to turn the spit by hand.

He could not sleep, however, but shivered and licked his bruises. The voices of customers coming and going drifted to his back corner, along with the tantalizing scents from the streets. He knew there were vendors out there with delectable items he had never seen, much less tasted.

He was sorting out the chants of a scissors grinder and a gingerbread seller when Nimrod came pacing across the yard, taking care to step around the puddles of slush. The cat settled himself nearby in a dry spot and began to lick.

"You know, dog," he said after a while, "there are times lately when you think like a cat. No, really. You didn't use to."

"Is that a compliment?"

"Of course. Well, I *know* you're a dog."

"Do you realize," Presto interrupted, "that I don't know any other dogs? Except Fuzz, that is."

"Fuzz." The cat spat the name. "He doesn't even make a

good animal. It all comes, I say, of spending too much time upstairs in the parlor with nothing useful to do. He puts on human airs. I can't understand," the cat continued, kicking vigorously behind one ear, "how an animal could lower himself so."

Presto said nothing but thought how neatly Fuzz could fit into the treadwheel.

"But that isn't what I came about," Nimrod continued. "I watched the boy mend the spoke. He tied it up with some twine, but really, it's nothing a few good bites couldn't take care of."

"Aaah?"

"Thought you'd be interested. Also, they were so impatient to get it back in working order that they banged it about a deal, and — well, I haven't examined it closely you understand . . ."

"Is it loose? Is it?"

"I believe so."

"Only one less spoke makes an exit."

"Will you take the chance, Presto?"

With the thought of escape so real and near, the dog felt suddenly afraid of the outside world, of which he knew nothing. But he knew about the wheel, and just as suddenly he felt the years clamp down on his constant useless running.

"Yes," he said. "Yes."

The cat smiled. "Splendid."

*

Presto didn't dare wait long to make his escape because he feared one of the humans might fix the loose spoke properly

12

after the day's work was done. Also, it was one thing to escape the wheel and quite another to get out of the building. Nimrod promised to stay nearby and create a diversion if necessary, but the best they could hope for was Presto's dashing through the upstairs guestrooms and finding one of the windows open.

There was little time to dwell on it, for the hostler came out, grumbling that his job was to mind the horses not mutts, and scooped up Presto by the scruff of his neck. The dog was thus borne into the kitchen and pushed into the wheel.

He braced himself against the swaying and saw from the corner of his eye that one of the outside spokes was wound with string. He took a few steps to bring it forward, and the hostler, who also had to set up the new spit, snarled at him to stop moving the fool machine.

Now with the broken spoke at eye level, he saw that the string was indeed carelessly wound. He licked it. When no one seemed to notice, he nipped the string and tugged at the big clumsy knot. It moved.

The hostler lost his grip on the spit of mutton and let it fall with a crash against some pots at the edge of the fire. He began cursing, and when the cook joined in, adding descriptions of his clumsiness, he increased his shouting and slammed outside. Presto could hear his voice trail across the yard.

The cook routed a scullery maid from the pantry, and, between the two of them, they managed to wrestle the spitted joint into position. All this gave Presto time to chew at the knot, but it was by no means loose enough when the meat was in place and the cook kicked the wheel to make him start it.

He began running, nervously aware every time the knot

flashed by, and trembled whenever humans passed lest they notice the string and think to tighten it.

The chambermaid came in with a guest's tray and asked after the hostler. The ensuing shouting match between her and the cook gave Presto time to stop the wheel and bite the string, but he dared not stop it long for fear the meat would start burning.

Fuzz came down for his usual handout. He sneered at Presto but took care to stay across the room. Nimrod, patrolling the pantries and larder, strolled through the kitchen often, glanced encouragingly at Presto, and flattened his ears at Fuzz.

The chambermaid was in and out, snapping sharp remarks except when the landlady herself sailed through, as she did with increasing frequency. Several Twelfth Night parties were expected, so preparations became more and more frenzied as the afternoon wore on.

Fuzz, who knew the kitchen staff would never reprimand him while his mistress was about, stayed underfoot and demanded tidbits whenever anything interesting seemed to be going around. It was the same situation with the landlord's nephew, who cadged sweets and rattled on about the Twelfth Night mumming he was going to perform for the family that evening and what a jolly costume he had for his role as the dragon and how he got to die when St. George stabbed him.

The cook remained unappreciative except for the bit about stabbing, but the turmoil and chatter gave Presto several opportunities to gnaw at the string. Now, as the wheel turned, a new sound added itself to the usual creakings. The split dowel, slightly loosened from its wrappings, moved in its socket, and Presto could hear its faint click as it passed his ear

14

on each revolution. When he was able to stop the wheel, he leaned experimentally against the spoke. It bowed out slightly, and he felt the flutter of freedom in his heart again. Then he noticed Fuzz staring at him from under the big work table. Presto started the wheel again.

The activity in the kitchen increased as diners began arriving. Servingmen rushed in and out with steaming dishes while the maids fled from cellar to pantry for forgotten ingredients. The cook shouted more than was usual even for her, and Fuzz took care to stay out of her way, though he did not leave the room as Presto wished he would.

When the roasting mutton was judged to be done, Presto had further opportunity to chew at the string while the people replaced the spit with another holding chickens. When Presto started again, he still held an end of the string in his mouth. As he walked the wheel forward, the string slowly unwound and pulled free from the spoke.

He heard a click as the spoke came around and shifted next to his ear, and at that moment he saw Fuzz regarding him, open-mouthed.

"You there," barked Fuzz.

Presto began running again, hoping the humans wouldn't notice. Fuzz kept barking, but the appearance of the landlord's nephew wearing a huge papier-mâché dragon's head occupied the staff's attention. He bounded through the kitchen door, growling and roaring. The younger, more giddy maids shrieked and dropped whatever they were holding. The cook, startled by the suddenness of the new annoyance, seemed about to clout him one with her ladle, but struck out at the shouting girls instead.

15

Fuzz leaped about barking, so Presto decided the time had come, and he threw himself against the split spoke with as much force as he could muster in so confined a space. The nephew stalked around the room, declaiming his lines in a muffled voice deep inside the mask, and made jumps at the maids as he passed to make them squeal.

"Break, break!" yelled Fuzz. "The turnspit is breaking out."

Nimrod appeared at the pantry doorway and took in the scene just as the hostler came in from the yard with a blast of cold air and a look of astonishment. Opposite him, the Otways appeared through the inner door and demanded to know the cause of the racket.

Their presence silenced the staff, but Fuzz barked on in the sudden hush and began capering toward the wheel, where Presto struggled desperately.

Nimrod saw this and gave a screech that lifted the chambermaid nearly out of her shoes and stopped Fuzz cold in midstep. With all eyes now on him, the cat bristled his fur, flattened his ears, and sank to a crouch. He fixed his gaze on the narrow space behind the plate cupboard and began to creep forward.

"Rats!" shouted the landlady.

The hostler stepped in and pushed the door closed behind him. But the strong draft that still flowed in to chill Presto on one side clearly indicated the door had not latched.

"Freedom," thought Presto, and grasped the spoke in his jaws. He shook it and felt it move in the socket. Nimrod was making horrible gurgling growls as he advanced on the cupboard, so even the dragon-headed nephew and Fuzz were totally absorbed by his actions. Behind them, Presto felt the last

16

fibers of wood splinter, and lifted half the spoke away. He let it drop and pulled out the other half.

As the pieces of wood clattered onto the flagstones, Nimrod leaped behind the cupboard and proceeded to battle the imaginary rat with all the noise of half a dozen cats.

Presto squirmed through the broken wheel and tumbled onto the hearth.

"Fake, fake," Fuzz shouted. "There's no rat there. Can't you *smell* that?"

But the humans were completely deceived, and the chambermaid took the opportunity to have a fainting fit. The hostler started to catch her but stepped on the cook's corns, and when she swung out with the iron ladle, she caught the dragon on the back of his head, and soon the kitchen was a tangle of overturned humans.

Presto dashed for the door and scrabbled at its edge, pushing himself through the crack. Fuzz nearly went hysterical when he saw the other dog actually loose.

"Get him! Get him!"

But the door opened sufficiently, and Presto was out of it in a flash. Fuzz forgot his position as lapdog and attempted to follow, but the nephew, bawling inside the dragon mask, stumbled over an upturned chair and fell against the door. It closed with a bang.

Outside, Presto shot across the yard and passed through the gate into the world.

CHAPTER III

*In which freedom's drawbacks are discovered and
some unsympathetic characters encountered.*

When Presto realized no one was going to catch him, he felt
giddy with relief, so dazed with joy he hardly knew the emotion was happiness. He ran, leaping and dodging, going somewhere, anywhere instead of around in the wheel.

He sprang into the crowding life of the streets among the
noise of peddlers' hand bells and street cries, through clouds of
scents both good and bad, past the heavy-footed dray horses or
between ill-tempered sedan-chair carriers, and over the sprawl-
ing beggars, away and beyond into the milling crowds.

By the time darkness came, he finally realized he was far
from Fortune's Whim, but just where he was, he had no idea.
Although he had spent all of his short life in London, he knew
nothing about the city.

Presto became more aware of his fatigue as the night's cold became more bitter. He needed a sheltered place to sleep, but the back streets were not encouraging. Rats loitered on the refuse heaps, and more than once he heard the voices of other dogs, which sent a chill along his spine. He pressed himself against a broken rain barrel when a burly pack crossed the end of the alley, silhouetted in the sickly light that dribbled from the cracks around doors, for there were no lamps here.

Immediately they were gone, Presto doubled back. The rats sat up and watched him with their level gaze.

He slept at last under a broken crate, dreaming of wheels. Toward dawn he was surprised out of sleep by a nip on the rump, and jumped across the alley before he was fully awake.

"There's a good pup," said a large hound. "Go along now. This is my crate."

"Can't I just rest a while?"

"No. Wouldn't think of it." The other dog sauntered over and, without the least trace of malice, nipped Presto's shoulder.

Presto yelped and ran in a circle. The other dog watched him with only mild interest. "Ah," he said, "you're new to the streets."

"I escaped yesterday."

The bigger dog nodded. "You'll have to see the Spotted Dog then."

"I will? Who?"

"Never mind. Just get going now."

"But how will I find him?" asked Presto, backing up and sidestepping another nip.

"You don't. He finds you."

19

*

Hollow with hunger, Presto made his way back to the main streets, which were already filling with humanity and noise. Schoolboys dawdled along in knots, swinging their book bags and throwing chunks of frozen slush at various targets, such as small dogs.

Presto dodged most of what they threw and had the satisfaction of grabbing the bread and jam one of them dropped while scuffling.

It was the merest mouthful, however, and he was still hungry when he found himself in a part of town where the wider, cleaner streets were not much use for scavenging. He came into a square where trim houses surrounded a small fenced-in park containing bare, symmetrical trees. It was much larger than the yard by the Fortune's stables, and Presto was amazed to see so much sky at one time.

Then, on a quiet side street of respectable lodginghouses, Presto caught a most delicious smell, one he remembered from the Fortune's kitchens — a chop. He spied a boy in a serving apron carrying a covered dish up the steps of one of the houses. This reminded him of the times when the odd-jobs boy would deliver a hot meal someone had ordered from the inn.

Presto followed and ducked behind the railings when the door opened. A very young footman appeared and reached for the tray, but the boy from the inn held on.

"I'm to collect the price of it first," he said firmly.

The footman, although no older than the other, evidently thought his livery and position put him a few notches above mere delivery boys, and made a haughty reply as he reached again for the dish.

But the delivery boy produced a paper from his pocket and began reading off a list of outstanding bills. The footman made an angry reply, and the delivery boy turned, with a shrug, to carry the plate back down the stairs. Presto caught the full scent of the covered meal and began drooling.

The young footman's anger got the better of his pretensions. He leaped down the steps after the other, and soon they were shouting a fine row. The man who owed the money leaned out an upper window and called some sort of reprimand down to his servant, but it went entirely unheard. The landlord ran out the door to inspect the racket, and all up and down the block curtains twitched aside as curious faces peered out the windows.

The lodger ran outside to stop the scene, but evidently he also owed his landlord, for the two of them had much to say to one another when they met. The servants, meanwhile, were about to proceed from words to blows. The delivery boy set down the tray with a clash and swung a right at the footman.

Presto could hardly believe his luck, but lost no time in taking advantage of it. While the humans were involved with the fight, the dog nosed aside the cover and grabbed the chop. He didn't like to leave the rest of the meal, but the man who had ordered it saw him and began shouting.

Presto shot down the street and up the first alley he found, doubled back behind the houses, and squeezed under a fence into someone's garden. He took the chop under a bush and devoured it with great satisfaction.

He rested a while out of the wind until he heard the clicking of several sets of dog claws.

"There he is, Ma. I told you I saw a stranger."

Half a dozen spaniel puppies peered at him through the twigs, jostling and yapping nervously. Their mother came forward to see, and they scrambled behind her for safety. "Will he bite?"

"Hush," she said, and then, addressing Presto, "You realize of course that this is our garden."

"Well . . ." Presto began, but one of the bolder pups, who had come closer to sniff, ran back to his mother yapping excitedly.

"He's the one we saw. The bone is there. The chop bone."

The pups bounced around and made little dashes at the bone in question. Their mother cocked her head and considered Presto.

"Ah," she said. "We watched you from the sitting-room window, you see."

"Oh, that. I hadn't eaten all day. Longer."

"It was cleverly done," she said in a motherly tone. "The boy oughtn't be so foolish as to put a plate of food on the ground. Are you still hungry?"

The pups were now making so bold as to worry his tail and make little feints and mock attacks. "Yes, I am."

"I wonder," she said almost to herself. "The butler was talking about getting a ratter. Terriers are supposed to be good ratters. How about you?"

Presto shook a puppy off his ear. "Well, I don't know. The rats I've seen are pretty big. I'm not so sure . . ."

"Aren't all terriers natural ratters? What do you do, then?"

"They had me in a turnspit."

"Oh, my. How degrading. But only for dinners, I suppose?"

22

"This was at an inn, so it was nearly all of the time."

"Well, at least you have experience," she said in a manner that to Presto seemed heartlessly ignorant. "Perhaps cook could find you a place. Besides," she added, ignoring Presto's agitation, "I can always use help with the puppies."

"I don't think so," he answered.

"Don't worry. It's no trouble to put in a word."

Presto leaped to one side, sending puppies flying. "I mean no. I cannot accept your offer. I must go now."

The puppies squealed, their mother looked shocked, and a maid come to fetch the dogs shouted at him to get out. He did.

*

He wandered aimlessly, finding himself in dingier neighborhoods as a fine snow began to sift down. Presto was still angry over the meeting with the spaniels, so when he and another scavenging dog both saw the same lump of suet, Presto did not draw back as he might have before, but lunged in, snarling.

"Ouch! No — Ouch!" the other yelped, and rolled away, though Presto knew he hadn't touched him. He gulped the suet and stared in amazement. The other, eyeing him from the far side of the alley, was a skinny mixed breed somewhat larger than Presto, but of such a cringing character that his tail seemed permanently pulled between his legs. The contrast made Presto feel bold.

"You mustn't mind me," whined the other. "It's just that foraging is so bad lately, and what with the cold . . ."

"What's your name, dog?" Presto asked.

"Me? I'm only old Beggar. That's what they call me. When you report to him, say . . ."

"Him? I don't understand."

"Why, Himself. The Spotted Dog."

Presto scented an extra wave of fear when Beggar said this, and remembered what the other dog had said that morning. "This is new to me. Who is this Spotted Dog?"

"You don't know? Oh my, oh my." He howled softly. "I am the least of his subjects. I don't dare take you to him. Oh dear. Will he think me lax? Oh dear."

"Perhaps," said Presto, "I'd better leave."

"No. Oh no. Wait. I see someone who'll tell you. Wait." He scuttled off toward a larger dog who was coming up the alley. The falling snow had obscured the scent of his approach, but Presto suspected by his attitude that he had been watching them. They both came back to Presto, Beggar cringing in the other's wake. "This is Lurcher," he said.

Lurcher said nothing, but sauntered stiffly around Presto to sniff him all over with the confidence of one who never forgets a scent. Presto stood like a rock, trying not to tremble, until the big dog backed off.

"You come with me," said Lurcher.

"Where?" Presto asked. Lurcher's eyes narrowed.

"Where?" Presto repeated.

Beggar fawned, saying, "He's new. He doesn't understand." The big dog looked as if he made no exceptions for insubordination, and took a step forward.

Presto ran.

He whirled around and headed for the street so fast it felt as if someone had begun the action for him. He could hear

Lurcher galloping after, and Beggar howling back in the alley as if he had been bitten.

Presto shot along, propelled by pure fear, leaping and dodging obstacles, bounding under and flying through with all his strength. But the big dog was longer legged and better nourished. People shouted and sprang aside. The beer wagon, however, could not. Its great horses shied but could neither stop nor turn. Presto ran between their massive shaggy hooves and was nearly clear when one horse nicked his haunch and sent him rolling. He couldn't see what happened to Lurcher since he was skidding on his shoulder toward a knot of people around a puppet show. He whizzed under the booth's curtain, smack against the shoes of the puppeteer.

The man yelled in surprise. Presto gasped and got his legs going again. It was not until many blocks had passed that he felt he had lost his pursuers and dared to slow down. Then, when he could collect himself, he realized the puppeteer seemed familiar.

Could it have been Dick Oakes?

CHAPTER IV

In which Presto and a human waif exchange mutual favors.

The snow tapered off when night fell, but Presto was so afraid of meeting more large dogs that he hardly dared stop anywhere. He came to a market area where people still milled about with the endless unexplained tasks humans always found to do.

The cold breeze carried a warm scent of pease porridge from the food stalls. Presto crept toward a trash fire, but one of the men warming himself there drove him away with a kick. So he kept on, thinking each flickering shadow hid a pack of dogs.

He felt desperate and befuddled. If he had stumbled into the yard of Fortune's Whim, he would have stayed and accepted his fate.

Presto turned and ran deeper into the tangle of back alleys. At last he had to stop, and heard, over the thumping of his heart, a whimper. He perked his ears forward — it was the sound of a human child.

A dingy shop front across the way had a display shelf projecting from its window, and under it, a number of children huddled against the cold. They were tangled together and wrapped in a variety of rags and old sacks, which made it difficult to determine how many there were, though he estimated four.

Presto approached. A leg in the bundle twitched, and one of the children sighed. The dog was cold enough to take the risk, so he squirmed between the sleeping forms under the tangle of rags. Some little warmth seeped from the shop's foundation, and, with this and their shared body heat, they slept.

Presto woke a few times in the course of the night, after the manner of dogs, to check for danger. On one occasion he opened his eyes to find the silhouette of a man hulking over them, leaning down, reaching . . . But before Presto could yelp an alarm, the man rumbled a comforting noise in his throat and allowed the dog to sniff his hand. Then, silently, he reached to tuck a coin in each sleeping child's fist.

He straightened up with a grunt and looked down, sadness showing in the set of his wide, stooped shoulders. Presto, feeling no fear of him, dropped asleep as the man turned away.

He woke at dawn to find the astonished face of a little girl gazing into his own. She held him tightly under one arm, much to the surprise of them both, and alternated between staring at him and looking at the coin in her other hand.

"Cor." She wriggled from the pile and sat up, still keeping

27

her grip. The other children muttered and stretched. One by one, they saw the coins in their hands and reacted, but only one was foolish enough to exclaim out loud. An older boy hit him and told him to shut it. He dropped the coin, and there was a scramble for the money. The girl holding Presto didn't join in, and when the shoving stopped the others saw the dog for the first time.

"Look, Margery has a dog." They looked at him as they had looked at the money.

Margery tightened her hold and Presto squirmed. The others gathered round, prodding him until he snapped.

"We can sell him," said the bigger boy. "I know a cove who always needs ratters for the pits."

But Margery had other ideas. Presto was amazed at the strength of her grasp. "No, Tom," she shouted.

"Look, Miss High-and-Mighty, we share what we get. Remember?"

Margery stepped back. "This is different."

The others sneered. The look in their eyes was not unlike the look in Lurcher's eyes.

"I don't want him sold to the pits. You know what'll happen. It's not fair. Would you sell Polly to the Beggars' Guild? You might get more for *her.*"

The other girl in the group wailed aloud at this, and Tom struck her across the cheek. Then he advanced on Margery. "I'm not going to argue. Give me the mutt."

Margery dodged away and ran up the alley. The two younger children shot after to head her off. She had her back to the wall and, since her arms were full of Presto, could only kick, which she did to some effect. Tom swaggered over.

"He's the first luck I've had in this rotten life," she shouted, and aimed a toe at his shin.

She connected.

There were fists and feet everywhere after that, and, with a convulsive wriggle, Presto sprang forth, to land running. With her hands free, Margery delivered a few good blows on the younger tormenters and stung the nose of the larger. It gave her time to escape into the street while the others hopped around in pain.

Presto saw her coming and sped along, running in and around carts and stalls. Several streets later, he paused to rest and, looking back, saw Margery still on his trail. The others were nowhere to be seen, but he started again and this time doubled back and forth among the alleys. He paused.

Margery was still in sight.

After this happened several times, they both sat to rest in an out-of-the-way court, eyeing each other cautiously. At least, thought Presto, she was different from most even if she had squeezed him. They spent the next few hours wandering about London, staying twenty feet apart from one another.

Margery appeared to accept the situation for the time being, though now and again she would call to him. Presto refrained from getting closer, however, and kept an eye on her as he poked in gutters and refuse heaps for food. Since he had to watch for cart horses and pedestrians as well as — more important, it seemed — the other roving stray dogs, he had a pretty miserable time of it.

He noticed Margery duck behind a wagon and slip up an alley when a group of ragged children came in sight. They didn't see her, but Presto watched and realized that while one of them begged from a passerby, the others picked the benefactor's pockets. Certain adults also seemed to make Margery nervous, but she was practiced at disappearing behind any available cover and so managed to avoid them.

As Presto gulped down a mouthful of something even he could not identify, he noticed a strange thing about Margery. She could walk past an object on a stall — an apple or a bun, usually — and it would disappear. Then she would continue walking at the same calm rate, and several blocks later the item would reappear in her hand and she would eat it as if it were nothing unusual.

Since Margery seemed likely to stay by him, Presto wondered if she might be of advantage to him, after all. Just as he considered allowing her to come closer, however, his thoughts were interrupted by a sharp, burning pain on his left ear. Lurcher was back.

Presto shied, but the dog held his grip, and it was impossible to get away without damage. He moaned quietly. The big jaws clamped on his ear without piercing it. He could feel the teeth on either side of the thin and tender flesh. The enormously controlled power was far more terrifying than any quick nip would have been.

A dirty little tangle-haired dog swaggered up to Presto. "My friend here says you refused his invitation yesterday. Now, that's not nice."

"What?" said Presto, trying not to move.

"You have to see the Spotted Dog. If you don't come when you're asked, we *make* you come. That's enough, Lurcher."

Lurcher let go, and Presto sidestepped away from his head.

"But why?" Presto demanded.

30

Lurcher grinned. "This is a cheeky one, eh, Crony?"

The shaggy dog was not amused. "Listen, cur," he said. "You come because he says so. That's all you need to know. Are you so impressed by the way the humans treat you that you can't bear to break away?"

"Well . . . no."

Crony's tone turned coaxing. "If we don't band together under the Spotted Dog, there's no hope for us separately. Those monsters are no good. It's us or them, I tell you."

"I'll have to think about that," said Presto, as he sidled away. But Lurcher was on him with a horrible snarl before he got anywhere. He thrashed about helplessly under the big dog's foot, when suddenly Margery was on Lurcher.

She came in yelling and hit him on the nose with a stick. He backed off in astonishment, but it gave her just enough time to grab Presto and hare off down the street with him under her arm.

Her sudden foray had caught the attention of passersby, and some of them now threw stones and lumps of ice at Lurcher and Crony, who retreated in the opposite direction. Margery kept running away from them, however, and didn't stop for several streets.

At last she collapsed onto someone's front steps and let go of Presto. He sat where she put him, looking at her admiringly. Then she reached over and folded him in a fierce hug.

"I couldn't let them hurt you. You're me *luck*."

He wriggled out of her grasp but did not run away. They sat side by side on the step regarding one another. She might, thought Presto, make an ally.

He perked his ears — footsteps.

31

Some children came around the corner and spotted them. Presto recognized the boy who had wanted to sell him. Margery jumped to her feet as quickly as the dog, but the others were too close and they had to stand their ground.

The others formed an arc to bottle their prey on the steps. They smiled as Lurcher and Crony had smiled.

"That's them, Major," said Tom.

Major was obviously their leader, a situation revealed mostly by his swagger and partly by the army hat he wore whose cocked brim still sported a few tatters of gilt thread. The rest wore ragged caps or just rags.

"Well now, Margery," he said. The others grinned, but Margery didn't answer.

"Are you too good for us now?" he continued. "Or do you mean to go in business for yourself, now that you've stolen that dog?"

"I did not steal him."

"Oh, I think you did. You certainly didn't share it."

"*He* was going to sell him to the rat pits." She pointed at Tom as if she wished lightning would come from her finger and strike him down.

"So?"

"You're all alike," she shouted. "I told you I wanted to quit."

Major laughed. "Quit!" The others joined in with a show of teeth and moved forward. Margery stepped back up the stairs.

Presto decided to act. He shot down and got Major by the ankle. The boy was so surprised, he stopped short and tried to kick the dog away, but succeeded only in kicking Tom, who was closer. They fell in a heap, and Margery leaped off the steps.

A couple of the girls in the gang jumped her, but Presto was around them like a whirlwind.

The door of the house banged open. "You brats get out of here!" A red-faced man shook his fist from the top of the steps, and a woman appeared behind him with a broom she evidently meant to use to good purpose.

The gang of children were not much impressed, but the distraction gave Margery time to break away and get around the corner, out of sight. Presto ran after her, with the others behind.

He moved in a blur, but after several turnings and dodgings he lost her trail. The gang still followed him, so he headed for the main streets and lost them among the market stalls and traffic. He paused, panting, to make sure they were gone. It was getting on to dusk; church bells were ringing the hour. He hoped Margery had escaped. That would make them even.

Street lamps glowed, and he proceeded from one pool of light to the next. The sky still held a dingy city-stained light, though it was dark between the buildings.

There was a clatter of hooves behind him and a ringing of harness. He shied. He was always getting in front of horses, it seemed. They drew a coach and, though he dodged, the driver pulled the reins so that the huge beasts turned and followed the dog. Presto was confused. He ducked through a gateway, but the horses and coach followed him there as well, looming large as nightmares. The place was an inn yard where the coach regularly ended its journey, but Presto was ignorant of that and continued to run before them, ahead of the nervous shaggy hooves. He yelped, and pelted straight across the yard into the stables.

The coach stopped outside, and Presto could hear the coachman swearing and yelling to the horses to calm down. The dog realized he was shaking all over.

There was a sound by the door. Presto whirled around to see a man just then entering. They stared at each other in surprise and recognition.

It was Dick.

CHAPTER V

*Wherein our hero, though swearing fealty,
discovers all is not well.*

They stared, each knowing full well who the other was, but
neither, at first, able to believe it.

"Presto?" Dick asked.

And Presto trembled, shifting his paws.

"It *is* you." Dick extended his knuckles for the dog to sniff.

Now that he had found Dick, Presto didn't know what to do
about it. But while he shifted from paw to paw in confusion,
Dick produced a heel of bread from his pocket and broke off
a piece. He tossed it on the floor halfway between them.

Presto ate without hesitation. Soon he was taking bread
from Dick's own hand while the man ate half the heel himself. When they were done, Dick rested his hand lightly on

Presto's head. Presto gazed up at his friend with eyes brimming with trust.

"Hmm," said Dick. "I think I've committed myself."

*

They passed the night in an empty stall, curled up on either side of a small chest containing Dick's belongings. The stable was relatively warm from the coach horses' body heat, and peaceful with their quiet rustlings and snortings — though one of them complained a bit about dogs who *would* get underfoot.

At first light, a stablehand banged through the door. Presto catapulted out of sleep, leaped over the box, and stood braced against Dick, barking furiously. Dick seemed more than a little startled by this commotion next to his ear, and bounded upright, clutching his head. The horses startled and looked around.

"Where did *that* come from?" the stablehand demanded.

It took Dick a moment to sort out the situation, but he placed his hand on Presto's back. "Quiet, boy." Presto, surprised by his own audacity, calmed immediately.

"Part of my act," Dick explained.

"He wasn't with you when you came. Say, isn't he the stray that got under the horses yesterday?"

One of the horses snorted disgustedly.

"Well . . ."

Presto remained by Dick's left foot throughout the conversation and kept an eye on the stableman. Dick had persuaded the innkeeper to let him hold his puppet shows in the courtyard. This would supposedly attract customers to the bar inside. In return for a place to sleep in the empty stall, Dick had agreed to handle certain chores while the odd-jobs boy recovered from a fever brought on by a Twelfth Night indulgence in strong liquors and preserved pears. It was assumed the pears had brought him low.

Now Dick's friend seemed unsure what effect the addition of a menagerie would have on his employer.

"One small dog is hardly a menagerie."

"To him it might be. Anyway, the odd-jobs boy is coming back."

Dick shoved his hands in his pockets and thought a moment. "One more day. Anyhow" — he grinned winningly — "today may be a success."

It was not.

The morning show was apparently too early to attract much of an audience. The noon performance followed the arrival of a coach and fared better, but the afternoon shows began dropping off. Most of the onlookers — there weren't enough to call them a crowd — were street urchins who, having no money anyway, ran off as soon as the curtain closed.

Presto observed all this from behind the flimsy canvas booth where Dick toiled. He took care not to get underfoot while the man waggled the puppets above his head over the edge of the booth-front in sight of the audience, himself unseen. He exchanged them like gloves for their entrances and exits, and talked all the while in an odd, high-pitched voice that was supposed to be the voice of the puppets.

The dog cocked an ear. It was rather confusing to him, as he was unaware how this was supposed to appear to the people out front. The little wooden-headed dolls did mimic the foolish ways of humans after a fashion, yet it was so obvious by the scent that there was only one living man inside the booth that Presto wondered just how much the audience believed.

The children, at least, enjoyed it, and screeched with laughter when the puppets belabored each other with slapsticks. The take, however, was small. Dick attempted cheery smiles as he passed the hat after each show, but few put anything in it. A well-dressed woman who had come on the coach with a little boy dropped in a shilling. The rest were coppers.

And that evening the odd-jobs boy returned.

Dick, leaving the kitchen with a bucket of slops, met him as he entered, pale and bilgy but ready for work. So it was their last night in the stable, and Presto curled close to Dick's sleeping form for mutual comfort. But Dick did not sleep well. Instead, he tossed wakefully, apparently wondering where to go next.

In the small hours, when everything had at last gone quiet, Presto woke suddenly, senses tingling. He knew someone else was there. But where? He strained his ears and hardly dared move lest he rustle the straw. It seemed a long time before anything happened, and then he heard a distinct rattle of dog claws approaching on the stones and stopping at the door. Someone snuffled at the sill.

Presto's hackles rose as he heard the breathing outside and the scratch of a paw on the wood. Then the wind sent a cold draft under the door and brought the scent of Lurcher.

Presto yelped, and Dick sat up like a shot. Even he heard the unseen dog. He threw a shoe at the door. "Gerradavit!"

The snuffling went on. Dick groped around and threw the next thing that came to hand. It hit the door with a thud and fell to the stone floor with a clang. They heard a low woof, and the dog moved off, but with no great haste. Presto heard him chuckling.

"We'd like some sleep back here," said one of the horses, *"if you don't mind."*

It seemed no time at all before the stablehand came in, bringing cold weather with him. He stumbled as he entered.

"What went on here? Is this yours?" He tossed Dick his shoe. "This one isn't." He held up a rusty horseshoe.

"Oh, that," said Dick sheepishly.

Presto stretched and scratched while Dick explained about the prowler. The stableman only shook his head and said the innkeeper ought to get a big dog of his own. Dick shook the straw from his coat and appeared to be considering this while he put it on.

"Could the landlord use a night watchman?" he asked. "Presto here gave the alarm last night."

The dog cocked his ears attentively and tried to look fierce. But the man only laughed and wished Dick luck as he stamped off to water the horses.

*

As they plodded through London, Presto was content to leave worrying to Dick. The dog, cold as he was at times, felt a certain inner warmth, knowing he had someone he could trust. He snapped at what scraps came his way in the streets, but the urgency of the days before was past.

Nevertheless, he could not help noticing that Dick had something of a stray's wary look. The few shows he performed at the edge of a market did not seem to encourage him.

Presto peered around the booth curtain at the audience's legs.

Except for some children who seemed to have no place in particular to go, most of the watchers, however much they laughed, stood for only a little while and then walked on. One gray shadow of a man did not. Instead, he hovered at the edges, taking care always to be behind the others. Presto saw him extracting purses from pockets.

But after the show even he left. Dick sat glumly in the lee of the booth, counting his few coins. He rubbed his head and stared at the tattered pattern of some old playbills fluttering on the wall opposite. Presto could tell by his eyes just when his attention suddenly fixed upon them. Dick stood up and went over to read them. There was quite an overlapping collection — old and torn, new and freshly pasted.

He stared at them closely, seemed to find something he was looking for, and paused to consider what he had read.

Presto growled. The pickpocket had appeared next to the booth.

Dick turned and scowled. "You, Dip."

"At your service. How's business?"

Dick stalked back and began dismantling the booth. "Well enough."

"Of course it is. That's why I couldn't be bothered to lift your purse."

"Your restraint is amazing."

"I'll just chalk this up to charitable expenses. But why be so stubborn? You know I'm willing to help."

"Stow it, Dip. I've told you before what I think about your kind of help."

The pickpocket sneered, showing what was left of his front teeth. Presto bared his own. "High and mighty, aren't

40

you? But I'm generous by nature. I'll buy the dog from you."

Presto's heart skipped a beat, but Dick fixed a withering gaze on the man and told him what he thought of that idea.

Dip sneered. "I'll be back when you've tried starving for a while." He slouched off and disappeared down an alley.

Dick threw his hat on the ground and kicked the folded booth. He went back and peeled one of the bills from the wall, moving his lips as he repeated the words to himself.

"Come on, Presto," he said, jamming his hat over his ears. "There's someone I have to find." He shouldered his gear and led the way.

CHAPTER VI

In which new allies are met,
both canine and human.

Their destination proved to be a tiny theater on the ground floor of a shabby building. They went down an alley to the stage entrance and stepped into the dim backstage confusion. An unseen audience thumped and clapped. There was a scrape of violins, and a tenor began a romantic ballad.

"You," a voice rasped from nearby. "Out. We have a show to put on." An old man stepped from the shadows.

"I'm looking for . . ." said Dick.

"We're not hiring now. Never hire puppet acts, anyway."

"The O'Connors," Dick insisted. "I'm looking for them."

"Why didn't you say so? But they're busy now. It's nearly their cue."

"Will you take a note to them, then?" Dick already had the

scrap of playbill handy, and rummaged in his pockets for a stub of pencil. The old man huffed and fumed, but waited while Dick laboriously wrote his message, and then took it off down a hallway and returned muttering. Dick and Presto waited uneasily, listening to the music.

Presto stiffened and braced against Dick's shin. At least a half-dozen dogs were approaching down the corridor, nails clicking, noses sniffing. Two humans walked among them.

"Dick Oakes," one of them called. The whole troupe surged in their direction. Presto shivered but stood firm.

"Hawkins here said you were looking for us," said Mrs. O'Connor. "You ought to have come sooner. We're so sorry to hear about your master, Old Cruft."

"Well, if you know each other," grumbled Hawkins as he slouched off. "Don't blame me if you miss your cue."

The other dogs studied Presto but made no move to attack. Mr. O'Connor listened, nodding agreement as his wife talked to Dick. Although the two of them wore gaudy stage costumes, Mr. O'Connor seemed as solemn as a basset.

The troupe of dogs cocked their ears when another flurry of applause came from the audience. A flushed young man strode in from the stage. "I think that went over rather well," he said, not to anyone in particular but more as a general statement. Presto heard Hawkins snort.

"Our cue," said Mr. O'Connor, speaking for the first time. Mrs. O'Connor told Dick to wait for them, motioned to the dogs, and led the troupe to the wings as the master of ceremonies announced them: "The O'Connors and their College of Canines."

"Too many dogs back here," the old man grumbled.

"How was I, Hawkins?" the tenor asked. "Perhaps a little more tremolo in the third verse . . ."

But Hawkins escaped into whatever cubbyhole served as his office, and the tenor went off to inquire in the greenroom.

Dick sat wearily on his puppet box to watch the O'Connors from the wings. Presto leaned against his leg and peered into the small stage, where the surging mass of dogs was separated from the surging audience by a glare of footlights. He could smell the melting tallow and the mixed scent of the crowd punctuated by the clean sharpness of oranges being peeled.

The Canines, with their humans, whizzed around in complicated group acts alternating with solos. For these, the dogs sat in a silent grinning line while one of them performed with a human. An elderly white West Highland terrier fetched, carried, and hopped in and out of baskets for Mrs. O'Connor.

Later, a poodle addressed as Voltaire posed reading a book, while a raucous tourist interrupted his work repeatedly, continuously protesting great admiration, until the dog chased him away. The tourist with his string of nonstop jokes and patter was Mr. O'Connor, whirling about the stage under an oversized wig.

When they all ran offstage to a satisfying round of applause, O'Connor sobered immediately, as if stepping out of a coat, and seemed more like a basset than ever.

Dick was on his feet, clapping loudly. "I can't believe . . ."

But the troupe was obliged to take a curtain call, and it was some while before they settled to talk in the dressing room.

"What are friends for, my boy?" asked O'Connor, as he removed a false nose. "Especially in our profession."

Presto leaned close to Dick and kept one eye on the Canines.

44

They seemed self-confident enough not to bite, but Lurcher and Crony were still on his mind.

Dick rotated his hat in his hands. "I don't want to impose," he said almost severely. "But Cruft *did* say . . . That is, times are so bad just now . . . Well, sometimes it seems the crossing-sweepers make more than I do, and then Dip got after me." He glared at the room and then looked down in confusion at the state of his hat.

"It *is* a hard life," Mrs. O'Connor said before he could add anything. "Our own boy wouldn't go into it. Not a bit. He finally took the King's shilling, as they say, and now he's soldiering in America. But our Lucy married a rope dancer," she added proudly.

Dick sighed but Presto stiffened, for the other dogs were approaching.

"You ought to have had more time learning with Cruft before going out on your own," said O'Connor. "A sad business that, his dying so sudden. Sad all around."

"He was a good master," Dick said. "He told me about his professional friends in London, but we had only just reached the city when he fell ill." Then he finally noticed the ring of dogs around him and Presto. They were coming up stiffly and according to rank to sniff Presto all over. Having memorized his scent, they wagged their tails genially. Presto found this a welcome change of events but was nevertheless grateful for Dick's reassuring hand on his head.

"Easy, boy."

"Oh, let me introduce you," said Mrs. O'Connor. She began sorting out names and faces for Dick, beginning with Trig, a fox terrier no larger than Presto but clearly the leader. The others were the French poodle, Voltaire; a Welsh corgi called Taffy; a black Aberdeen terrier named Charles Edward; and the motherly West Highland terrier, Flora Macdonald.

"Welcome," Trig said. He was not a biter.

Mrs. O'Connor smiled at the troupe. "We'll be glad to help you train Presto for your act, Dick. *Won't* we, Trig?" she added, and Trig thumped the floor with his tail.

"The stage?" said Presto. "Well, I don't know that I can . . ."

"You'll like it," said Trig.

"Of course, dear," said Flora. "If the O'Connors think so, why, then, you can do it." She sniffed Dick's ankle. "Yes, we can trust this one."

Then the other performers began coming in, to disappear behind screens and emerge dressed like ordinary people. Over their chatter, the dogs heard Hawkins shouting from the stage door.

"I don't need any urchins hanging around. Now get out!"

The faintest cold draft made its way down the hall as the door slammed shut. Presto was not sure, but thought he caught Margery's scent.

There was little time to wonder, however, for the O'Connors were leaving with their dogs. Mrs. O'Connor said their good nights to the other performers and gathered the Canines about her with a brief command. Presto crowded close to his human, and Dick stumbled.

"I think," said O'Connor, "we will need to learn heeling."

Although the other dogs politely ignored the mishap, Presto felt acute embarrassment and watched each step so closely that they were soon past Hawkins — still grousing over the number of dogs he had to put up with — and into the alley.

"Now, we can recommend you to Mrs. Lightfoot at the Punch Bowl," Mrs. O'Connor said to Dick. "She lets a few rooms. I think, O'Connor, you ought to take Dick Oakes there this evening."

"Yes, my dear."

"And ask after that job you heard of."

"This is most kind," said Dick. "I don't want to be any trouble."

"I'm sure you'll find a way to return the favor," said O'Connor. "I don't want to hear any more about it."

Presto sniffed and started as they left the alley. Lurcher had been there and deliberately left his scent on the corner as a threat. Trig noticed, too, but did not remark on it. Presto continued to peer into the alleys they passed and sample every breeze. He was just as glad, when the party divided and they left off Mrs. O'Connor and most of the dogs at their rooms, that Trig was going to accompany O'Connor with them the rest of the way.

"You'll find the Punch Bowl interesting," said Trig. "Our friend Bouncer works there, to keep order. The owner is Mrs. Lightfoot, a retired wrestler — formerly Hannah the Hammer."

"Oh," said Presto. It sounded like a safe place to live.

"Street entertainers like to gather there," Trig continued; "small-time performers like us. Not the grand types from Drury Lane. Very reasonable rates and no funny stuff. Needless to say, pickpockets and their ilk don't go there."

The Punch Bowl was marked by a sign swinging over the entrance with the name emblazoned on it in chipped gilt letters. Above this was painted a huge china bowl in which sat

47

Mr. Punch the puppet, leering crookedly and waving a jaunty salute to the patrons passing below.

Everyone inside seemed to know O'Connor and called greetings as they walked the length of the big plain room. Presto began to panic. There were several dogs sitting by their masters, and every one of them was looking at him. In addition, the scents and sounds reminded him of Fortune's Whim, and the sudden recollection of his captivity came back like a shower of sleet.

Trig noticed his trembling. "I know these dogs. Besides, Mrs. Lightfoot doesn't allow fights."

"The wheel," Presto murmured. He kept his eyes on a sizable hound by one of the booths lining the wall. The four of them progressed among the tables toward the bar at the back, where food and drink were dispensed.

"Good evening, Mrs. Lightfoot," said O'Connor, and Presto looked up to find himself at the feet of a large and formidable woman. Humans, he had noticed, came in much less variety than dogs did, but in general the females were smaller than the males. This woman, however, was a good head taller than any man in the room, and had an air of calm power.

O'Connor introduced Dick, who snatched off his hat and ducked his head in deference. They inquired about a rented room, and O'Connor added some details about Dick's struggling career. All the while, Mrs. Lightfoot coolly scrutinized the applicant. As humans didn't sniff introductions, Presto wondered what clues she looked for, but when they finished speaking, she smiled, shook Dick's hand firmly (he winced in surprise), and said the back upstairs rear was available if he didn't require much room.

"Bouncer," she called. Presto jumped. A big elderly setter came around the bar. "Bouncer," Mrs. Lightfoot continued, "these two will be staying here. Put out your hand, Dick Oakes." Dick did, to let the setter sniff his knuckles. "Now you," she said to Presto. Dick held him while he snuffled Mrs. Lightfoot's hand. As large as she was, Presto sensed kindness from her.

Then he was set back on the floor so that Bouncer could sniff him, which he did with slow deliberation. The setter then looked up at his mistress and grinned.

"Fine," she said. "I'll have Betty clear out that room, and we'll show you up later."

"Evening, Trig," said Bouncer, moving off on his rounds among the tables. "You too, Presto."

The humans discussed rent with Dick, who explained how erratic his earnings had been. "I'm willing to work for it," he explained.

Mrs. Lightfoot considered a moment. "Not much call for it here. Ned takes care of what Betty doesn't do. But there's a cow house a few streets over, where we get our milk. Do you mind shoveling manure?"

"I grew up on a farm."

"Then I'll speak to the milk woman when she comes tomorrow."

Once that was settled, O'Connor took Dick to a table and introduced him to a number of professional acquaintances. All these new people were beginning to confuse Presto. He was glad to ignore them — there seemed to be no danger — and merely take his ease under the table with Trig and the one other dog of the party.

"This is my friend Presto," Trig explained. "He's new to the trade but learns fast. Presto, this is Bob."

They touched noses. Bob was a smallish mixture of hounds, all black except for a patch on his chest.

"Bob's master, Wilcox," Trig continued, "is blind. So Bob is his eyes."

"Also his nose, Trig. Don't forget that. But most humans are nearly blind in the nose anyway, poor creatures."

"What does your master do?"

"Sells ballad sheets. He memorizes them and sings 'em off to advertise, but between us, he sings like a hinge." Despite the criticism, Bob was clearly proud of his human and, for all his smallness, very protective of him.

The shoptalk went on both over and under the table. But fascinated as he was, Presto fell asleep and didn't wake until nearly everyone had gone. O'Connor was bidding Dick good night, and Bob and his man had already gone upstairs to their room. Betty, the maid, wiped the empty tables while her husband, Ned, who constituted the rest of the staff, ran a mop over the floor.

Mrs. Lightfoot loomed into view. "There is one thing I insist on. The dog" — she pointed at Presto — "must be bathed. There's water in the scullery."

She disappeared into the kitchen. "Now?" Dick asked. He seemed as sleepy as the dog.

"Yes," said Betty. "She means now."

Presto hadn't the first idea what they were talking about, except that it concerned him. He trotted after Dick into the kitchen and watched doubtfully as Betty poured hot water into a wooden tub.

She handed Dick a rag and a firkin filled with soap. "Now don't douse the whole room."

Presto yelped when Dick lifted him over the steaming tub, and squealed when he was dunked, protesting, up to his shoulders in the water. He whined and moaned, but Dick held him firmly and worked up a lather all over his grimy fur.

"I'm trying to be careful," said Dick, but some of the soap ran into the dog's eyes when he poured on the rinse water.

Presto howled.

A blast of cold air hit him as the back door flew open to slam back against the wall, loosing a furious little figure in a flutter of rags.

"You stop hurting him!" shouted Margery.

CHAPTER VII

Wherein former strays embark on new careers.

None of the humans in the room had ever seen Margery before and had no idea what to make of her now. Since no one moved, the girl made a snatch at Presto, who scrambled out of the tub, trailing soapy water across the floor. Glad as he had been for her friendship in the streets, he had no intention of leaving Dick.

"What's all this racket?" Mrs. Lightfoot filled the inner door, with the smaller figure of Ned behind her. She scooped up Presto in one hand and held Margery by the other.

Margery was undeterred. "I want me dog back!"

Mrs. Lightfoot raised an eyebrow. She kept a firm grip on the girl's collar and handed Presto to Dick. "Dry him before he catches his death."

With considerable relief, Presto stood still for a rubdown with a bit of clean sacking.

"He appears quite another dog," said Betty. Dick fondled his ears approvingly. His fur was now definitely white with honey-colored patches over the ears. To his own surprise, Presto even felt better clean. Comfort was still new to him.

Margery squirmed but could not get free. "Now you, my girl," said Mrs. Lightfoot. "Who are you?"

"He's *my* dog."

"What?" said Dick.

"Your name."

"Margery Daw," she muttered. "He's me luck. And I'm *not* letting you put him in the pits." She lunged, but Mrs. Lightfoot plopped her onto a bench and held her there.

"The pits?" said Dick, astonished.

"You're all alike," the girl yelled. She kicked the bench leg and gritted her teeth in a tremendous effort not to cry.

"I'd never . . ." said Dick.

"Where did you get that idea, my girl?" asked Mrs. Lightfoot gently.

Margery struggled to escape, but even a grown man would have been hard put to break Hannah Lightfoot's hold. The girl was unable to choke back the tears any longer and burst into a noisy, wailing cry.

Presto stepped forward and licked her hand. He could think of nothing else to do.

"So he does know you," said Mrs. Lightfoot.

Margery strangled on her tears but managed an answer. "We dossed under a shop front, and when we got up next morning we had glanthem — a win each — and I had the dog, too. And that was the first luck I *ever* had, and I don't mean to lose it."

Presto, startled, crowded close to Dick. Mrs. Lightfoot continued to consider Margery. "My dear," she asked, "what lock do you cut?"

Margery looked at her feet. "I knuckle," she muttered.

"Hmm. Prigging wipes?"

"Yes. *Yes.*" Margery jumped up. "And lully-prigging, too. I have to do *something* for bub and grub."

"Sit down, Margery." Margery sat. "I can well believe you have had a hard time of it . . ."

"What do you know . . ."

"You keep your dubber mum! I know more about what goes on in the streets than you suspect. I've seen plenty of girls like you. Now listen. There's honest work here for you if you think you're up to it. *If* you can keep your daddles out of the till."

Margery looked confused, so Mrs. Lightfoot continued. "If cleaning doesn't suit you, maybe one of the troupes that stop here will take you on if you've a mind for the stage. But if you want to go back to your old ways, you'll be out on your ear. Understood?"

Margery nodded and swallowed.

"Well? Will you try it here?"

The girl looked around the room as if checking for exits. She looked hard at Presto. "Will *he* be here?"

"Yes. They've just moved in."

"Then I'll try it."

Mrs. Lightfoot smiled.

"I didn't understand a word of that," said Dick.

Margery looked him over in surprise. "Green, isn't he?"

"Fresh from the farm," said Mrs. Lightfoot.

*

Presto soon accustomed himself to the new routine of their days. He and Dick awoke in the winter dark of their tiny room under the eaves, where the roof slanted sharply over the bed, and the single dormer window framed a pair of pigeons grumbling about the cold.

Dick opened the door, and Presto ran down the stairs to the kitchen, where Betty or Ned let him out into the yard. One thing he had been taught at the Fortune, after a ruined roast, was how to be housebroken.

Once Dick got the job at the cow house, he usually went there first and ate later. Presto accompanied him only once. The dim barn full of bored cows made him nervous. They stood all day, every day, in their stalls, surrounded by the city, and reminisced incessantly about green fields. Yet the place was better managed than some in London. "You be thorough, now," the manager told Dick. "This isn't one of those cow houses where the beasts stand in their own mess until their tails rot off. I'm keeping my eye on you."

So Presto preferred to stay at the Punch Bowl, which pleased Margery. The girl, as Ned explained to Dick when he asked for a translation, had admitted to Mrs. Lightfoot that she was a pickpocket and had stolen handkerchiefs and laundry put out to dry. But she was being given a chance at an honest job here as long as she kept her hands out of the money box and passing pockets.

Indeed, she seemed to be settling in well enough, and Presto's presence was perhaps her greatest incentive still. It was true that Betty had had more trouble with Margery's first bath than Dick had had with Presto's. The girl remained wary of the people but had the alarming habit of grabbing Presto and hugging him fiercely.

The humans were mystified by Margery's account of how she met Presto, not so much that the dog came in the night, but that money had appeared — a penny for each child, enough for breakfast. "In my experience," Dick observed, "money usually disappears."

*

The rest of the mornings were spent training with the O'Connors, who, in addition to the room they rented at the rear of a large house, had a fenced-in area perfect for practice. When Dick and Presto arrived the first time, the Canines were outside, kiting around and barking steam to work the night's stiffness from their joints.

O'Connor whistled them into line and regarded their devotedly wagging tails with his usual grave expression. Then he called his dogs forward one by one to practice their basic moves. Dick sat on an upturned keg with Presto between his feet and watched intently. The Canines frisked through rolling over, fetching, walking on their hind legs, and turning somersaults. When each had done a turn or two, O'Connor dismissed them for a rest period and came to sit by Dick.

"Never work 'em for too long at a time," he said. "Then end it off with something you know they do well. That encourages 'em."

Dick nodded and reached down to scratch Presto's head.

"How," Presto asked Trig, who trotted up to join them, "how can you remember all that?"

"One learns." Trig looked pleased with himself. "Just what does your Dick Oakes have in mind for you?"

"Nothing like that, I hope." He began feeling panic at the thought of trying to remember so much. "Doing something with puppets. The dog one got broken, you see."

"Hmm. I've heard of animals performing with puppets but never known one who had. Very interesting. But you're lucky," he added. "Many masters aren't as patient as ours. They would rather push the lessons forward by fear." He growled and put his ears back. "Like Madam Midnight and her spectaculars — dog soldiers defending and attacking a burning castle, with *real* fire. *Ha.* There's none of that nonsense here, I'm glad to say."

Dick, meanwhile, had been clasping and unclasping his hands. "Mr. O'Connor," he said. "You are taking a good deal of time and effort with Presto here . . ."

"The trouble with you, Oakes," said O'Connor, "is that you can't let anyone be even mildly generous toward you. You get as prickly as a hedgehog."

Dick flushed. "I've accepted *too* much from people."

"So if you want to repay," O'Connor continued, "you can help by fetching and carrying for a new show we're preparing."

"Yes?"

"We're combining with a few other acts we know — a singer, comedian, juggler, clever pig, and so on — and renting a small theater. We do *not* need a puppeteer. But we could use a hand backstage. This would still leave you time to go on with your own puppet shows, of course."

Dick looked relieved. "I accept." He turned to Presto. "Come on, boy. Time for work."

Mrs. O'Connor came out to take charge of the other dogs, and Presto's apprenticeship began.

"Just watch me," said Trig. "He'll say a thing, and then I'll do it. Once you get the connection, it's easy."

Presto cocked his head and watched. O'Connor said, "Stay," and walked across the yard. He turned, waited a bit, and then said, "Come." Trig trotted to him and was patted. Then the man said, "Heel, Trig," and the two of them walked around the area, the dog staying close but never underfoot.

"These, plus some fetching," O'Connor said, "maybe walking on the hind legs, *and* stage presence, and you have it. I think we'll start with sitting."

Having Trig to watch was a help, although Dick had to use more than words at first. "Sit," he commanded. Presto smiled up at him without moving. "Sit," Dick repeated, and pressed firmly on the dog's hindquarters until he sat, with a thump. Presto scrambled to his feet, unsure of Dick's meaning since there seemed no circumstance to require it.

Dick sighed and persisted.

However, by the end of the morning, Presto began to get the hang of it. He received bits of biscuit when he obliged immediately, but Dick seemed so happy when Presto understood and obeyed that the dog was more than willing to please.

*

As soon as Presto mastered heeling, he accompanied Dick on

his afternoon performances. He sat in the booth away from Dick's feet and watched his human glove his hands with puppets and wave them over his head. Since he could scent that the things were not alive, he still wondered what the amusement was for the audience out front. But it was the audience itself that occupied most of his thoughts. He peered at them through a tear in the curtain. The way they gathered around the booth, staring, made him nervous. It was too much like the formation hostile dogs used, or the mob of children who had attacked Margery.

Presto preferred evenings at the Punch Bowl, when he could relax with Bob and Bouncer while Dick and Bob's Mr. Wilcox talked shop above them across the table. And there were usually others to stop by: the O'Connors and Trig; a juggler tossing up and catching bright balls while he spoke; young Jonet, who sold lavender and other herbs in season; and a magician, who, if the conversation lagged, might produce the Queen of Hearts from behind the girl's ear.

Margery was much in evidence, fetching and carrying. She had seemed offended that she was expected to wash her face and hands every day, but accepted the obligation in exchange for some clothing, which, though bought secondhand, not only fit her, but was in good repair and had been washed in recent memory.

She still acted furtive, however, so Ned and Betty never set her a task near the cash box. Betty took to counting the spoons every evening.

*

Presto passed through the taproom after closing time one

evening just as Ned found Margery examining a cocked hat.

"Give it here," he said.

"*I* found it. Hands off."

"What do you want with a man's hat? Now give over."

"I mean to sell it, not wear it," she said scornfully, eluding him as they circled the tables. But she hadn't noticed Presto and nearly tripped over him. This gave Ned the chance to twitch the hat from her grasp and hold it out of her reach.

"Lost items," he said, "go on a peg in the kitchen until the owner comes for 'em."

"Ha. What if he doesn't?"

"This one always has, and you need a talk with Mrs. Lightfoot."

It was the first of many such talks. When Presto passed the landing near Mrs. Lightfoot's rooms, he often heard her calm firm voice and Margery's shriller excitable one.

Nevertheless, the number of spoons remained constant, and only a loaf now and again went unaccounted for. But when Margery felt confident that meals would not be withheld and realized that the mice became too interested in anything she hid, this situation stopped.

There was the occasion, however, when Ned missed a crown piece. Betty questioned Margery cautiously at first, tearfully later. Mrs. Lightfoot looked sorely disappointed, and Ned raged. Bouncer declined to enter the room.

Margery stormed at them all. "I don't need your favors. I can be a mud lark and scavenge coal down by the river. Or I can sift dust in a dust yard, or I can go back to picking pockets. You all think I do, anyway."

Mrs. Lightfoot stormed right back. "And when you're older,

girl? I know what life in the streets is like. I was there. But I had a skill — fighting. So I didn't have to sell myself for a meal like the other girls. And I was strong enough to get rid of anyone who tried to persuade me to. What protection do you have, girl?"

Margery stared. "Why do you care? Nobody cares."

But Presto had seen a gleam of light between two floorboards and interrupted the quarrel by scratching at the spot. Ned saw him, hesitated, then knelt and flicked out a coin with the point of a knife. It rolled across the room in front of them all.

Mrs. Lightfoot was the first to speak. "Margery, I am truly sorry."

Margery said nothing. Next day, she set a small blue and white jug on Mrs. Lightfoot's breakfast tray. When Bouncer told the story later to the other animals, he described how touched his mistress was by the present and then, when she realized the girl had no money, began to doubt.

"That's a lovely jug, Margery. Where did you get it?"

"Oh, I prigged it from a stall. It's only secondhand."

"Margery, Margery. I asked you *not* to steal."

"You said I wasn't to steal from here or from the customers. Don't tell me you have *more* rules."

CHAPTER VIII

In which trouble hounds Dick.

Lessons continued with the O'Connors. Trig's example and friendly encouragement proved a great help as Presto learned "sit," "stay," and "come." "Lie down," "fetch," and "roll over" were more complicated, but the whole business was so interesting, and Presto so eager to please Dick, that soon he had a whole repertory to run through.

Dick placed a stick in Presto's mouth and persuaded him to approach with it. "Give," he said, and when the dog merely grinned around the stick, blew in his face. Presto dropped it in surprise but after a few tries would let go on command.

While he rested, he watched the other dogs rehearse their acts. Trig and Taffy had a new one, with O'Connor playing the part of an inept angler who kept dropping his poles and his hat. Every time he bent to retrieve a fish pole, one of the dogs dashed up his bent back, snatched his hat, and ran behind him to drop it before the man could turn to see what was happening.

"Not bad," said O'Connor. "Now try it faster."

They began again, hesitated only a few times, and soon ran through it at top speed, props flying in all directions as the dogs whizzed about like shuttles.

Trig, panting slightly, joined Presto. "That's a good one. We have some sham fish to use on stage that slither wonderfully."

They watched Charles Edward and Voltaire balance on the ends of a plank set across an overturned keg, silently concentrating on their footing while O'Connor solemnly presided over the act as if it were a weighing of souls.

*

Now that his evenings were spent discussing the craft with others of his profession, Dick's act by degrees began to improve. Presto, still observing from behind the booth, noticed audiences more apt to laugh and less likely to wander away without paying. Perhaps, the dog thought, it wouldn't be so bad to perform, at that. Applause certainly had a lively effect on Dick, whose mood perked considerably at the sound.

Along with other rehearsals at the O'Connors', Presto was persuaded to perch on objects of various heights while he watched the others practice. Although apprehensive at first, he was a nimble dog, and soon felt confident enough to sit on a stack of kegs or on a board between barrels. O'Connor, meanwhile, advised Dick in the building of a small shelf for Presto to stand on that would fold up when the puppet booth was disassembled.

Trig turned three backward somersaults and landed under Presto's perch. "Stop worrying." He barked, and danced away on his hind legs.

*

One evening at the Punch Bowl, Presto realized Dick's laughter came easier these days. He put his chin on Dick's shoes and settled down to enjoy the sensation of being surrounded by friends. The O'Connors were there, Wilcox, and Jonet.

"The Clive," O'Connor reminisced. "Now *there* was a comedienne."

"How about you, Dick," said Wilcox. "We all knew Old Cruft. How did you meet him?"

With some hesitation, but much encouragement, Dick began. He told about life on his father's small farm and about his five brothers and which of them joined the army or emigrated as a bondservant, which moved away to a city or continued on the land as someone's hired help. He himself, he said, met his fate at a country fair — a tiny thing where gimcrack booths were set up among the sheep and cattle pens, and sharpers wagered on which walnut shell hid the dried pea.

Old Cruft was there with his puppets, and Dick, having just driven one of his father's unwilling pigs to this market and then haggled over a price, forgot his tiredness and irritation and laughed louder than the rest at Mr. Punch. Even now, while he told the story, he showed the same excitement.

He talked with Cruft and came back the next day. "I hardly slept," he said. "There were too many new ideas." The old

puppeteer took a liking to him and offered Dick an apprenticeship. Dick's father was not at all pleased about it. There had
been some stormy scenes and much talk about coming down in
the world, but his father knew as well as he how few opportunities there were at home. So off he went, with his parents'
reluctant blessings and their admonitions to steer clear of
rogues.

Dick had gone with Cruft from fair to fair all that summer,
always on the road, practicing in every spare moment, taking
to the life as one born to it. "London this winter, my boy,"
Cruft had said, and told him of his friends there. Then the
old man caught a chill. He died in a shabby inn just outside
London, tended only by Dick, who, though he spent every
minute with his master, knew none of Cruft's friends nor
where they might be reached.

"So I saw him buried as decently as I could afford," Dick
said, "and came on alone into London, fresh from the country
straight into this hive. It was weeks before I found any of
Cruft's friends — I saw the O'Connors' names on a playbill by
chance. My luck really began to change when I met faithful
dog here." He reached down to pat Presto. "Isn't that right,
boy?"

Presto sighed in contentment. Then he saw a stranger's
shoes approaching, and his human friends suddenly fell silent.
Without waiting to be asked, the newcomer deftly swiveled a
chair over from the next table and straddled it to face the
company.

"Oh. Good evening, Sligh," said O'Connor, coldly.

"Hello, all," said Sligh, in a poor imitation of cordiality that
ignored O'Connor's tone. "And *this* must be Dick Oakes him-

self. I've heard a great deal about you. I knew your late master, Cruft."

"Yes, we met once at a fair. I expect you wouldn't remember . . ."

"You must be coming up in the world," Sligh interrupted. His smile, as if borrowed, seemed a few sizes too small.

Trig sniffed his ankle and growled. Sligh jumped — he hadn't seen the dogs under the table — and O'Connor said, "Sit, boy," firmly, but not as a reprimand.

"Who is he?" Presto asked.

"He's bad luck, that's what." Trig's hackles were still ruffled. "No one likes him."

Sligh stayed and stayed until the others made excuses to go, and the evening came to an unsatisfactory conclusion.

*

The matter didn't end there. Next morning, Margery appeared in the kitchen door while Dick sat outside on the stoop, cleaning the cow house off his shoes. She plunged abruptly into the subject. "That Sligh last night . . ."

Dick looked at her in surprise. She hadn't said two words to him since the first night. "Yes?"

"Well, watch out for him." She leaned down to pat Presto. "Since you're a friend of Presto's . . ."

"What do you know about Sligh?"

She shrugged. "I've seen him with pickpockets and footscamps. Especially one called Dip. He told him he was a puppeteer, but I never saw any puppets."

Dick was silent a moment while he fastened his shoes. "He *did* have a puppet show, but he wasn't very good. Had no heart for it, Mr. Cruft told me, and I dare say he doesn't. I met him a few times when he came around trying to borrow money. I think he actually *pawned* his puppets once."

"I thought I'd best tell you," she continued, scratching Presto's chin. The dog, though listening, had his eyes blissfully shut.

"Thank you, Margery," he heard Dick say. "Daw, you said your name was? I met a Daw with a horse act. Any relation?"

She frowned and began twisting the hem of her apron. "No. I gave myself the name. My mum used to sing me a rhyme about it."

"See-saw, Margery Daw?"

"Uh-huh. I was already Margery." She scowled at the muddy dooryard. "It's about all I remember except when she died."

She tried to say it lightly, but Presto caught the true tone of her remark and put a paw on her knee. That, and his soulful gaze, proved too much for her, and she collapsed forward, hugging him close both for comfort and as a shield for her tears.

Since she seemed to wish it, Dick made no comment, and after a pause merely said, "You must have seen a deal of trouble in so short a life."

She straightened up and wiped her nose on her sleeve. "I'm older than I look."

"But how have you managed?"

"Oh, Old Bett across the way took me in and taught me a trade."

"That was kind."

"Cor, no. She wanted one more for her pickpocket gang. She wasn't too bad as long as we kept her in gin. There's a lot of that," she added, seeing Dick's surprise. "I guess coming from the country you wouldn't know. Bett took only little 'uns. She couldn't handle the older ones, and we'd go off in gangs of our own. I didn't really like it, though. Then I met Presto."

"What do you want to do?"

"Don't know." Presto could feel, through her hand on his head, that she tensed, unused to talking so much about herself.

CHAPTER IX

Wherein Presto debuts and repays an old debt.

Margery, Presto decided, must have confided also in Mrs. Lightfoot. Although the landlady's own rooms were strictly off limits, Presto became consumed with curiosity and one day paddled stealthily down the passage to an open door, where he heard the two talking. It wasn't easy to keep his claws from clicking on the wooden floor, but neither human seemed to hear him. They were sitting in a sparsely furnished parlor whose wallpaper was hung with a patchwork of broadsides. Mrs. Lightfoot sat in a wing chair listening to Margery. The girl held a small wooden paddle and was sounding out something written on it.

"Ab, eb, ib, ob, ub." The knuckles that held the handle flickered white with concentration.

"See here."

Presto whirled around and saw Bouncer. "Oh, I'm sorry."

"You get back where you belong." He escorted the embarrassed Presto down the hall to the stairs.

"I'm sorry, Bouncer. I heard Margery and . . . What was she doing?"

"Learning to read. There now, my pup. Your little friend is fitting in quite well. Quite well indeed. Confidentially," he added, for unlike his mistress he was not apt to be close-mouthed, "it's a good thing the girl came. Herself was feeling down about her granddaughter."

"Oh?" It was a surprise that anyone that imposing could have problems.

"Mrs. Lightfoot's daughter doesn't want her little darling to be influenced by a former wrestler, she doesn't. Daughter fancies she's come up in the world since she married a shop-keeper. One of *the* Branghtons of London, as she'll tell you, as if that meant anything, or if anybody cared. She needs a good nip, that one."

*

Now, during Presto's acting lessons, Dick would put up the booth and run through his act while Presto sat on the new shelf at the edge of the stage. At first he only watched, to accustom himself to the puppets, which could be alarming so close, especially Punch, who whacked the others with his stick. But Presto could see Dick down inside the booth and trusted the man not to let the puppet touch him.

He soon learned the sequence of the play. Punch quarreled with Judy and tossed their baby out the window when it cried.

A constable came to investigate. "I come to take you up," he said, and Punch answered, "I come to knock you down." There was such a deal of knocking down and hitting that Presto wondered why more than the dog puppet hadn't been broken.

His own part came when Punch argued with his neighbor Scaramouche over who owned the dog. Punch, of course, claimed to, but Toby Dog would only growl when called and finally bit him on the nose. This made Presto very excited, and he began wagging his tail. Dick had taught him to growl on cue and would whisper the command from down in the booth. As O'Connor told them, it was a tricky turn, since you didn't want to teach the dog bad habits he might continue offstage.

In his excitement, Presto forgot a few times what Dick wanted and, instead of confronting Punch, ducked his head below the level of the stage to stare imploringly at Dick. But soon he responded to the cues so smoothly that he growled and bared his teeth at Punch most menacingly, adding a few ear-splitting yaps for good measure.

Then he could sit back out of the way and watch while a raucous Punch contended with a Distinguished Foreign Gentleman who, unfortunately for himself, could say only "Shalla-balla" before being knocked down. At last the hangman caught him, but the wily Punch talked him into demonstrating how the noose worked and thus hanged the hangman himself. This part was most effective, for when Punch hauled the rope, Dick slipped his hand out of the hangman puppet and let it snap up, to dangle limply.

Even when the Devil appeared to drag Punch off to the Land of Bobbety Shooty, Punch thwacked the Devil with his stick and rode offstage on his hobbyhorse, singing. For his own part, Dick added some comments and asides on contemporary issues, which worked well with some audiences.

"I think," said O'Connor, "that Presto is ready to perform."

*

Dick chose a side street for their first act together, one sure to produce an audience but not so busy that Presto need feel overwhelmed. The dog paced nervously over the cold cobblestones while Dick assembled the booth and arranged the puppets inside it on their proper hooks. He felt a little bilious and tried to remember what Trig had said about even the best having stage fright.

"Here, boy." Dick beckoned him over and held out his costume. Mrs. O'Connor had sewn him a dog-sized neck ruff for a present. "There, now." Dick fastened it and patted Presto reassuringly. "Very elegant."

Then Dick went out front and began chanting an advertisement for the show. Presto licked his dry lips and hoped he wouldn't be sick. When a sufficient crowd had gathered, Dick ducked into the booth, ready to begin. Presto looked up at him in misery. "You'll be *fine*," said Dick. He picked him up and gave him a quick hug. "I'll be right here, you know."

Then he drew the stage curtains apart and lifted Presto out onto the ledge. The booth seemed at least twice as high in the street as it had during practice. There was a mass of faces turned toward him. He gasped. But they were smiling, delighted at the sight of a live dog on a puppet booth. Punch popped up and began squeaking his lines. Presto tried not to

72

look at the audience, hoping that would make his head feel less tight.

"Growl," Dick whispered.

Presto growled without thinking. The people laughed. He cocked his ears in surprise. As he continued growling and barking on cue, the audience made more noises of appreciation, and Presto began to warm with a not unpleasant feeling. He could make these people laugh. When, at last, he bit Punch's nose, the crowd shrieked with delight. He grinned back, tongue lolling.

"You great ham." Dick laughed from the booth and afterward praised him well for his work. The crowd had been noticeably more generous, too, and Presto had no desire to stop.

For an afternoon show they moved to a market area where plenty of maidservants with shopping baskets, and apprentices on errands, dawdled long enough to watch them. Presto finished his number and was sitting back quietly when he heard a furious screech followed by high-pitched feline cursing. He stared over the crowd, craning his neck to locate the voice without leaving his place. Some human jeering was mixed with the screeching and the awkward clopping of tiny hooves.

There was a one-story lean-to sprouting from a shop across the way, along the slanted roof of which a cat slithered and stumbled to keep just ahead of some laughing boys. His ears were flat back against his skull, his tail hairs on end in a thick brush, but his claws were useless to him — half a walnut shell was tied to each paw.

He lost his footing entirely and tumbled off the roof to the street. Presto could not see him behind the crowd, but one of the pursuing boys yelled something about how he'd landed on his feet. Another shouted back that they ought to see what the beast could do if dropped from a window.

Without stopping to consider, Presto flung himself forward and landed running. The crowd gasped and parted. Dick called out in astonishment to see the dog disappear from his perch, but Presto was already across the street, barking and nipping at the boys' ankles. The audience, which at another time might have laughed at the cat's plight, were amused instead to see the performing dog make the urchins dance. For the boys had to do some fast and fancy stepping to get around Presto, who seemed to be everywhere. One of them snarled and shied a stone at him, but they disliked being the butt of others, and took the first opportunity to mizzle down an alley.

The cat had wedged himself between two baskets of cabbages to bite at the bonds. As the last walnut shell fell away, he caught his first clear sight of Presto. "You?"

"It *is* you, Nimrod," the dog said. "Quick. Get over here." He escorted Nimrod through the audience, which gave a round of applause, and into the booth. The cat got behind the puppet box and hissed at Dick. "You can trust him," said Presto, and then, seeing the man's surprise, touched his shoe apologetically.

Dick had seen Nimrod before, back at Fortune's Whim, but the big cat was bedraggled now, and Presto wasn't sure how much the man understood of the matter. Dick seemed to remember the cat, but the coincidence was too much for him, and he simply allowed Presto to bring his friend home with them.

The cat insisted on slinking behind every available bit of cover, especially when they passed groups of noisy children. As

74

soon as they reached the Punch Bowl, Nimrod shot across the taproom and went to earth in the recesses of the pantry. Even Bouncer was taken aback.

Dick explained what he could to Mrs. Lightfoot but had to admit himself baffled. Fortunately, she had a sensible attitude toward animals and gave orders that the cat not be disturbed until he was ready to come out. Nimrod clearly needed to compose his dignity. A few hours later, he consented to accept a dish of milk and some scraps from Betty. He ate this meal in a corner of the kitchen but still switched his tail in annoyance.

Presto sat nearby. "What happened?" He couldn't imagine his old friend getting the worst of a situation.

"They kicked me out — a couple of days and nights ago."

"Whatever for?"

The cat looked up. "I was observed trouncing Fuzz. It was almost worth it."

CHAPTER X

*Which contains improvement for some
and trouble for others.*

Next evening after work, Dick inquired about the cat.

"Well, he isn't here," Betty told him. "His High-and-Mightiness stalked out the back door this morning with his tail up. That's the last we'll see of him."

But when supper was ready, the cat was by the pantry door.

On the second day, since the weather was milder, Nimrod was observed from time to time sitting in the area beyond the kitchen stoop, his back to the door. Ostensibly, he was studying sparrows, but his ears, more often than not, were swiveled toward the inn.

At the end of the third day, he came up from the cellar with a dead rat in his mouth and placed it before Mrs. Lightfoot. Betty shuddered. Bouncer looked offended.

Mrs. Lightfoot glanced at the rat and then said, "Thank you, cat. I think you'll be earning your keep until we find you a home."

"First an urchin," muttered Ned. "Now a cat."

*

Nimrod settled smoothly into his new job with only a little coolness between him and Bouncer, who made it clear that *he* had seniority.

One evening the animals were sitting together, out of the way, after finishing their meals. Nimrod licked himself with a cat's slow thoroughness. "Very good," he remarked as he brushed an ear with his forepaw. "My compliments to Betty."

Bouncer glanced his way. "That's an odd accent you have. Rather more than a purr, isn't it?"

Presto cocked his ears. He didn't know any other cats, so he assumed they all spoke with a burr.

Nimrod stroked his other ear. "It's Scottish. My family is from the Highlands. Quite a story there." He continued washing.

Bouncer shifted impatiently. "Well? Aren't you going to tell us?"

"Yes, please," said Presto quickly. He could see the cat was about to tease the old dog with bits and fragments, if he wasn't urged along. "You know all about me, but I don't know any of your adventures."

"Well," said the cat, "I came to Fortune's Whim as a youngster and left, after years of unappreciated service, a short while ago."

Bouncer snorted.

77

"The story belongs to my parents, really." Nimrod sat up, curled his tail around to his front paws, and began. "My mother was a modest tabby who grew up in a genteel vicarage. My father, on the other hand, was a great Wild Cat, who roamed the moors and denned in a cairn where an ancient human chieftain had been buried. During one full moon he ventured near the village and saw my mother strolling in her garden. It was love at first sight . . ."

"Oof," said Bouncer. "This sounds like one of those dreadful novels Mrs. Lightfoot's daughter reads."

The cat flattened his ears and glared. "So they eloped to the heather and spent the days and nights of the full moon among the ancient stones and waving grasses, harmonizing wild Highland songs.

"My mother returned to the vicarage to see her family, fully intending to rejoin her love on the hill. But the people were moving to London. She was thrust into a box, and, although she called and called through its air holes, she doubted she could be heard far over the noise of coach wheels.

"She never saw him again. When they got settled in London, I was born, to the humans' surprise. She told me I much resemble my father."

*

Sligh kept coming back, inserting himself among Dick's friends, hinting he would accept a drink if anyone cared to stand him one. Presto would have preferred to avoid the man, but kept close to Dick. He came out of a half-doze one evening when Dick exclaimed, "But I can't give them up." He perked his ears.

"Well, now, I'm afraid they never were yours to begin with." Sligh sounded as if he were smiling.

"But I never borrowed money from you. How . . ."

Sligh tilted his chair back on its hind legs. "Mm. But Old Cruft did, you see, and put up his puppets as security."

"That doesn't sound like him. He never mentioned it."

"Perhaps he didn't want his apprentice to lose confidence in him. At any rate, he died before he could pay the debt."

Dick's friends spoke up angrily. Wilcox banged the table top, making both Sligh and Presto jump.

"Is it possible I could inherit my master's debts?" Dick seemed doubtful.

"What I mean," said Sligh, "is that Cruft forfeited the puppets for nonpayment. Therefore, they belong to me. I know you have been using them as if you had properly inherited them, but I won't make trouble for you. Just hand them over. You're doing so *well,*" he added — Presto could imagine the sight of the sneer he heard — "that you should have no trouble at all getting a new set."

Dick stood up. "I don't like the sound of this. Why didn't you mention it before?"

Some of the others got up, too, as if on signal, and when Presto came out from under the table to stand by Dick, he could see Sligh inching toward the door.

"I'd want to see something in writing," said Mrs. Lightfoot.

"Well now," said Sligh, "maybe you will."

*

Sometimes Presto felt so exhilarated by his newly won accomplishments that he seemed to be treading a few inches above the pavement. He hoped it would go on forever, but it ended one morning even before breakfast.

He had just awakened and was stretching luxuriously when he realized Dick, too, was awake, one hand pressed over his eyes, muttering, "Sligh, Sligh, Sligh."

Presto jumped to the bed and floundered across to lick Dick's ear. Dick half-smiled at him, and Presto realized, surprised that it could be so, how worried his human was.

And later in the kitchen, when Dick had left for the cow house and Nimrod was preparing to examine the cellar, Margery came in the back door, crying. Her apron was torn and marked with the clear impression of a muddy boot print. Her dress was likewise streaked, and the cap was gone entirely, letting her hair fall in her face over a layer of tear-stained mud.

She tried to push past Betty, but the woman caught the girl's shoulders. "What *happened?*"

Bouncer slipped out to fetch Mrs. Lightfoot, who appeared as Margery began bawling in earnest. To Presto's amazement, and Betty's too, by her expression, Mrs. Lightfoot picked up the weeping girl and held her tight. And equally surprising, Margery clung to her like a monkey until she had cried herself out. Then she was able to give a halting account of how, as she was on an errand, the gang she had escaped from found her and rolled her in the mud. Presto well remembered how she had hit and kicked their escape from the same lot, but this time they had ambushed her in greater numbers.

"For putting on airs, they said. But I didn't. I didn't even see them until they were all around me, and that Major knocked my cap off."

"To some people," said Betty, sniffing, "being clean is putting on airs."

"You wash yourself, my girl," said Mrs. Lightfoot. "Then come to my parlor for lessons."

"Reading isn't going to help now," wailed Margery.

"I don't mean reading."

*

Presto now approached his performance with a sober determination to do well. He still loved the laughter and applause he could produce, but now he had the vague feeling that his efforts could help Dick, and he took his responsibilities seriously.

Nevertheless, he could not give his whole attention to the matter. One day, as he gazed over the audience from his perch on the stage, he saw some large dogs leering at him from behind a cart. Another time, he was sure he recognized Crony, and nearly toppled backward into the booth.

*

Mrs. O'Connor suggested that Presto could pass the hat after a performance. "A basket, I mean. Something with a handle. That ought to get their attention."

Dick agreed, and Flora, who did an act that involved putting things in and out of baskets, volunteered to help. She demonstrated prettily, holding up her head so that the basket wouldn't drag.

Between practice sessions, Presto told Trig about seeing Crony.

"You want to be careful," Trig said. "They're persistent." But beyond that, he could offer no advice. On the matter of Sligh's threats, however, he sounded more hopeful. "Your Dick Oakes has friends — people who knew Old Cruft. They're not going to take Sligh's word by itself."

*

And all along, preparations for the O'Connors' show continued. A small stock of made-over scenery cluttered the O'Connors' kitchen until the theater would be free. The performers jointly composed a handbill during a long evening at the Punch Bowl, with considerable ill-nature displayed between the singer and the comedians. After the bills were printed, Dick and Presto went about pasting them to walls over as much of London as the supply allowed.

The theater itself was a small room behind the Sock and Buskin tavern. When it was ready, Dick trundled the scenery to it in a handcart. Presto stayed out of the way while the humans wrestled the flats and drops in place. He talked with the Educated Pig, who was, he learned, incensed at being last on the handbill.

"I never saw such small print," he huffed.

Presto sympathized but kept an eye on Dick, who was discussing something with the pig's trainer and showing an animation the dog found heartening. The problems with Sligh were as persistently in Dick's mind as a flea in the ear. But now he was occupied with his craft, and the fascination of it showed in his eyes and in his movement. Had Dick been a dog, Presto thought, he would be sniffing the air.

CHAPTER XI

*In which our hero encounters
the Spotted Dog.*

Everything crowded in at once. Instead of the pleasant anticipation of the O'Connors' opening to fill his thoughts, Presto
found himself worrying about Dick more and more. Sligh
didn't dare show his face in Mrs. Lightfoot's tavern, but he
spoke to them on the street more than once.

Then Margery came home with another bloody nose from a
run-in with Major's gang, just as Presto and Dick were leaving with the puppet booth. It put Presto's timing off during
the show, and afterward, while Dick dismantled the booth, he
was still so preoccupied, he didn't notice the ambush until it
was too late.

Three big dogs closed in and herded him away before he
could gather his wits. One loomed close, breath hot in Presto's

face, making it clear there must be no outcry. Dick saw none of this. But by then the dogs were in an alley, running silently. If he hesitated or even seemed to resist, one of his captors would nip his ear or haunch, and make no effort to be gentle about it.

The lead dog was Lurcher, who sneered when Presto recognized him, then hurried them on even faster. Presto realized, when he scented the same cook shop for the third time, that Lurcher was doubling the route back on itself, to avoid pursuit and confuse the prisoner. Once, when they paused in the shadows to let some swaggering men go by, he tried to sniff a marking post for clues. A guard shouldered him abruptly and growled.

They went on until Presto lost all track of time and place. They may have been near the docks when they finally paused behind a warehouse, but he was no longer sure. He felt dizzy from fear and fatigue, but not panicked. Instead, he observed events almost as if they were happening to someone else.

Lurcher sniffed the air and advanced up the alley, listening. A row of bulkheads led into the cellars of the warehouse, yet the locks were so rusted that stains from the metal ran down each slanting door.

Nevertheless, Presto was nudged toward one of them and saw that, behind a drift of trash, the wooden side of the bulkhead was rotten and splintered enough to allow even the big dogs passage. One of his captors eased through; then Presto was pushed forward by the second. Lurcher stood guard and came last.

Presto stumbled down the stairs into a brick corridor, going by scent and sound in the darkness. There was a dusty smell of grain somewhere and then, on a sudden draft, the scent of an alarming number of dogs. He stiffened and got nipped again. They went up some stairs, along another corridor, and finally paused by an arched doorway. A low murmur and scuff of dogs moving about stopped abruptly when Lurcher stood in the doorway and announced, "It is done, Your Lordship." He jerked his head, and the jailers hurried Presto into the room.

As he rounded the corner he was vaguely aware of a high-ceilinged vastness full of dogs staring at him, but he skidded on the stone-flagged floor, scrabbled for balance, and lost his footing entirely. He slid the last few feet on his shoulder and fetched up against a stack of crates.

Crony snickered nearby. The other dogs followed his lead, and the whole room buzzed with muttered laughter. Presto jumped to his feet and saw, for the first time, that he had landed under the gaze of the Spotted Dog himself.

This dog was not laughing — indeed, he seemed incapable of it. He was a big mixed breed with the smooth, wedge-shaped head of a bull terrier. Presto had to meet his small, piercing eyes only once to know they were mad. Nevertheless, the dog sat as erect and still as a statue and looked directly at Presto. Such a level gaze was both a test and a threat. Presto dropped his head but didn't dare move any further.

The Spotted Dog stood up. From the corner of his eye, Presto could see how he had gotten his name. A number of brindled splotches marked his sides. They seemed to form a picture of something — a shadow or a map — but there was no clear definition to them, as if the thing represented had blurred or else never fully formed.

The Spotted Dog stepped down from the dais of crates, not

even looking when Crony scampered aside to give room. He stepped onto the flagstones and stood above Presto.

Presto could feel his breath and was fully aware of the stiff-legged swagger of a pack leader. Just as he was about to look up, his feet were knocked out from under him, and he landed on his back.

It was so sudden, he froze, too witless for resistance. The Spotted Dog had a forepaw on Presto's chest. He bared his teeth.

"So, you don't like to take orders, do you? You think you're above that, eh? You'd rather toady to the humans, would you?" His voice was so soft that all the dogs in the room were silent in order to hear him.

Each quiet phrase sent a cold chill crawling between Presto's shoulder blades. He couldn't answer. But the Spotted Dog didn't want answers, and his questioning continued, emphasized now and again by pressure from the paw on Presto's chest.

"Maybe you want to be a lapdog, eh? Maybe you like being kicked around and then awarded the honor of licking your master's boots? Right, cur? Right, puppy?" The voice went on and on, but Presto could hear little over the buzzing of fear in his ears.

The pressure was removed from his chest. The Spotted Dog had moved to one side, not smiling even now but with a satisfied glint to his eyes: his authority had not been challenged. Presto rolled onto his stomach but remained in a crouch. The Spotted Dog took a stance with forefeet on a box and raised his voice to address the assembly.

"Fellow dogs. You see how our brothers are cowed, how

accustomed they become to oppression. They are treated like curs, and they begin to *think* like curs."

The dogs murmured agreement, some in heartfelt tones, some too quickly, as if fearing dissent. Presto thought he recognized Beggar's whining tones nearby.

"We have herded their flocks," the Spotted Dog went on. "We have fought beside them in battle, have guarded their dens and their young. For centuries we have done this and more. And what do the humans do for us? We are turned into the streets, or shot if we are not abandoned. And beyond that, we are made to kill even our own kind."

The dogs moaned and growled, though the facts were evidently well-worn with retelling. One young hound began barking his pent-up anger until an older dog knocked him down to silence him.

"You see?" said the Spotted Dog softly. "Even here we must creep about to avoid detection. The humans could be anywhere, listening."

The dogs sobered and sniffed around warily.

"Ah, Crony," said the Spotted Dog, and Crony hurried forward, tail clamped low, bowing with his forequarters. "Crony, I don't think our new member knows the story." He sank back on his haunches and let the smaller dog take the floor.

Crony glanced sharply at Presto and then addressed the room in a singsong recitation. "Our Leader was the strongest of a strong litter. From puppyhood, his ability to lead a pack was proven, yet he was cruelly taken from his family and sent to the pits."

Presto winced at the thought, but the Spotted Dog remained impassive.

87

"Here he was set against other dogs, goaded and tortured by hireling humans until he had to kill his own kind or be killed." Low growls came from every corner of the room. "And he *did* kill. And men became rich, wagering on the deaths of the dogs he killed.

"But his owner was overconfident. Why ought the dog to love him? Yet he took our Leader from his pen one day to exhibit before some idle sporting men. The door was left untended. The men were weak. Before they could gather their wits, our Leader knocked them down and sprang away to freedom."

Presto knew the feeling and exulted at the thought. The other dogs yelped aloud. When the room calmed, Crony continued.

"Since that day he has worn no man's collar. Never again will he submit under a human hand. Once free, he became wise in the ways of city streets and gathered about him a loyal band of dogs. Indeed, he became the Lord of London's Dogs, and under *him* we withstand our common enemy."

Presto had to admit he felt impressed. All the stories he had heard about human atrocities crowded back into his mind. Yet something was not yet right, and when the Spotted Dog turned to look directly at him again, he felt a chill of fear.

"Yes," said the Spotted Dog, advancing, "that is my story. We band together against *them,* you see. There can be no traitors." He was very close, and his little eyes showed the pleasure he felt in terrorizing Presto. "You *will* be joining us, won't you, puppy?"

Presto shuddered and turned his head to bare his throat. It seemed to go on forever before either of them moved. Then the Spotted Dog nearly smiled. "Crony," he said, "see that your new brother feels at home." He trotted out briskly, with a pair of the larger dogs closing ranks behind him in a neatly practiced maneuver.

"Welcome to the pack," said Crony, in a mildly sarcastic manner. "Now let's introduce you to the other members." Presto, hardly recovered from the interview with the Leader, had to stand still while every dog in the room came to sniff him all over and memorize his scent. Some were threateningly thorough, as if they expected to track him someday. Others were nearly friendly, and a few, like Beggar, cringed up to sniff and shy off, as if expecting a nip. Their rank was evident from the order of their coming.

"May I go now?" Presto asked finally.

"Go where?" Crony snarled. Back to *them?* You're one of us now. You'll stay the night here."

There was nothing he could do about it. The room's two doorways were guarded by sizable hounds. Most of the dogs left once the meeting was over, and those in charge didn't encourage loitering.

"One or two at a time," Crony was saying out in the passage. "It's dark enough now, but don't go all at once. And use the different exits."

Beggar slunk over. "I told you you had to see the Spotted Dog," he said from the side of his mouth. "Himself doesn't like to be crossed."

"How long do I have to stay here?" asked Presto.

"A few days, until he's sure of you. We all had to. Most of us."

"But the others?"

"Oh, we live in the streets as usual. This is just for meetings. All the stray dogs of London must pledge loyalty to the Spotted Dog. And . . ."

"I am *not* a stray. I have a human."

"Please. Be quiet," Beggar pleaded. But some other dogs heard and came over.

"He has a human," one of them said.

Beggar ran out.

Presto backed against the crates. The others were not much bigger than he, but it was one against four. They began circling Presto as much as the crates would allow, chanting: "Lapdog, lapdog." He had to look sharp to keep track of them all, and soon they got behind him one at a time and began nipping. When he whirled to face the biter, another moved in, and in a very short while all four were snarling and kicking on top of him. Presto gave bite for bite as well as he could until the mastiff on guard sailed in and tossed the four attackers aside.

"His Lordship's not through with this one yet," said the mastiff to the four as they limped off. It was clear to Presto he would have only as much standing with the pack as he could fight for. "Come on, you," said the mastiff, and urged him into the corridor.

Presto scurried ahead, favoring his left foreleg, until they came to a door blocking the end of the passage. "You doss here until Himself wants to see you again. And don't make noise. I'm warning you."

For a frantic moment Presto expected the Spotted Dog to appear through the door. "What's in there?" he asked.

"That's the working part of the warehouse. The humans store grain in there but they don't come to this part of it. That is," the mastiff added with a show of teeth, "they won't if you keep your mouth shut. Their drunken watchman knows someone lives here, but as long as we keep down the rats he doesn't try to find out."

"Oh," said Presto.

The mastiff looked amused and trotted back down the corridor to where the guards lounged. At least with them there, the other dogs wouldn't bother him. He listened hard at the door — not a sound, only the musty grain scent he had noticed earlier.

He turned around a few times and curled in the corner to get what sleep he could. The dim corridor soon darkened completely, and the dogs had to depend on scent and sound alone. But except for a distant scuffle between a guard and a rat, nothing happened.

Presto continued to doze and wake until the dingy light of morning seeped in. He stretched and shook himself, determined to face whatever came.

Nothing came.

The guards changed shifts down the hall. A few other strays passed through. Presto paced for a while, licked his wounds, and then dozed some more. He used one corner to relieve himself in, the other for sleeping. Boredom began to combat fear.

When the day was nearly over, a hound he hadn't seen before led Presto down the passage and around the corner to a place in the foundations where water seeped in. It was brackish, but Presto lapped up what he could before he was herded back to his corner.

That night he thought he felt a draft coming under the locked door, and heard a distant footstep. But when he woke fully both had stopped. Presto wondered about the watchman.

Next morning, while he was worrying about Dick, who could have no idea what had happened, a frowsy water dog approached and dropped a bone at his feet. It was well gnawed already, but Presto sprang on it eagerly.

"Compliments of Himself," said the water dog.

The rest of the long day was enlivened only when a high-ranking bitch on an errand flattened a guard for making rude remarks. But for the most part little happened. By the scent of the place and some subdued sounds, Presto estimated that only a few dogs were present at any one time. Occasionally he caught the scent of the Spotted Dog going about in other corridors, and then Presto shuddered all over until he had to shake himself to make his hair lie flat.

Early next morning, he felt the draft again. He sniffed at the crack under the door and scratched at the wood, but only once, because the hound on duty saw him.

"You," the guard barked. Presto froze. "Himself wants to see you."

And the Spotted Dog was there, at the far end of the corridor, still as a stone. The hound motioned Presto to approach and be quick about it, then retreated with the other guards to a respectful distance.

Presto walked the length of the corridor by fits and starts. He had no wish to get close to the Spotted Dog, but if he dawdled or paused, one of the guards would growl. He stopped a few feet away from the Leader.

"Well, puppy?" said the Spotted Dog. "Have you decided to break away from your human oppressor?"

It took Presto a moment to realize this meant Dick, and he felt hot anger replacing cold fear.

"I love Dick Oakes."

The Spotted Dog said nothing. The pupils of his small eyes shrank as if to concentrate their madness. He opened his mouth. Presto was sure the Leader intended to kill him, yet he meant what he had said, and braced his paws for whatever might come.

Something banged against the door at the end of the passage.

All the dogs turned to stare, and saw light seeping through the cracks around the jamb. A rusty grating noise came from the keyhole, and the guard dogs stepped back. A human voice on the other side of the door said, "Force it, if you have to. I'll not buy what I can't see."

The guard dogs shifted their paws and gazed imploringly toward their Leader. The noise changed to the thumping of a shoulder against wood.

The Spotted Dog licked his lips. "So that's what you were doing. Scratching and pawing at that door . . ."

"No, I didn't . . ." Presto ducked the teeth but was knocked down before he could finish, and fell, breathless, against the wall. There was a confusion of legs as the guard dogs jumped over him, colliding in their haste. He heard barking and yelping from the meeting room and saw, when he regained his feet, a number of low-ranking dogs running in confusion.

The door opened with a bang, and the watchman fell through. Behind him two better-dressed men stood gaping in astonishment at the swirling mass of dogs. One held up a lantern whose harsh light and shifting shadows sent one young mongrel into complete panic.

The other man, who had spoken of buying, demanded answers the others couldn't give him. The dogs were now escaping by every route they knew, and Presto ran with them. He nearly took a dead end but scented, as he paused trembling in one dark hallway, a stream of outside air. He followed it and found the broken bulkhead around the next turn. The escaping dogs were so intent on their own safety that no one bothered with him.

Presto ran as hard and as desperately as when he had escaped the wheel of Fortune's Whim. He ran until he was too tired and then he walked until he found familiar landmarks, and trailed back to the kitchen door of the Punch Bowl.

Betty was emptying slops when he dragged into the yard and collapsed.

"Bless me," she said. "It's Presto."

CHAPTER XII

*The hero returns and friendship
foils villainy — for a time.*

When Presto returned, Margery hiked up her petticoats and
sprinted off to find Dick. The two of them came back at a
dead run, to find the dog installed in a flannel-lined basket by
Mrs. Lightfoot's parlor fire.

Presto struggled from his blanket and flew to meet his human. Even the cat later admitted it made a touching scene, as
the man held the dog, who licked his chin. Neither could get
enough of the other's sight. Presto felt Dick draw a deep
breath and let it go as if ridding himself of something very
heavy.

Indeed, everyone at the Punch Bowl tended to him, though
all he needed was food and sleep. Mrs. Lightfoot salved his

wounds and allowed him to spend the next few days in her parlor while Dick was out. It was all very luxurious.

He was surprised at how concerned everyone had been. Betty and Ned were in and out during the course of their duties, with kind words and treats. Margery fussed protectively, and even Bob and Wilcox appeared at the door. Nevertheless, Presto wished he could be out with Dick, performing.

Nimrod and Bouncer kept him informed of current gossip, and he watched Mrs. Lightfoot drilling Margery in her lessons, which now included, besides reading and ciphering, self-defense.

"Put your hands up, girl. No, not so far. You're wide open."

Nimrod, who went where he pleased, joined Presto by the fire and watched the girl bob and jab an invisible opponent. "She's improving," he said. "All her lessons were off while you were gone."

"Really?"

"I don't think Dick had much sleep then, either. When he wasn't working, he was out looking for you. I don't know how he managed with the O'Connors' show, but I hear it succeeded."

Presto had forgotten all about that. "Oh, dear."

"There was," said the cat, "a remarkable amount of rejoicing when you came home alive. I suppose humans have feelings after all."

They watched Margery shadow-box for a while until Mrs. Lightfoot said that was enough for the day. "I heard something about the girl," said Nimrod, "from an acquaintance who got it from a friend who . . . Well, anyway, you remember you said a man gave pennies to Margery and the other urchins?"

"Yes. I was the only one who saw him."

"That seems to have been some writer called Samuel Johnson. His cat, I was told, overheard him muttering to himself about the children. He goes for long walks when he can't sleep, and when he sees children like Margery, with no place to go, he wants to help them. But what can he do? There are so many of them. He himself had to live in the streets for a time as a young man. So he gives them something to buy breakfast with. He must have a kindly nature. All his cats spoke highly of him."

"The children really have no place to go?" asked Presto.

"No more than you or I did."

Mrs. Lightfoot pointed to the notices tacked on the wall. "This was my first professional match," she explained to Margery. " 'And sundry others.' I was one of the sundry others on the bill."

"Did you win?" asked Margery.

"Easily. And these over here are when I had a name for myself. 'Hannah the Hammer.' But I prefer these, from when I married my manager."

Margery spelled out the line of bold type. " 'The Celebrated Mrs. Lightfoot.' Cor. Is that you in the picture?" She pointed to a small oil painting over the hearth that showed a sturdy young woman poised to fight.

"It is. A Mr. Hogarth did that. The silhouettes on either side are of Mr. Lightfoot and myself, a wedding present from his sister. Very handy with shears, she was. Made a passable living from it. And speaking of family," she added, leaning to rub Nimrod's broad skull, "we have to be thinking about a home for you."

When the humans had left, Presto asked, "How *is* that coming, Nimrod?"

The cat twitched an ear. "She was talking about her daughter's family. They live over a chandler's shop and could probably use a mouser."

Nimrod seemed doubtful about the idea, so Presto dropped the subject.

*

In honor of their show, which bid fair to have a goodly run, the O'Connors decided to hold a celebration dinner at the Punch Bowl for all concerned, and bespoke the small private dining parlor for the occasion.

Presto, who considered himself fully recovered, happened to be passing through the kitchen as Betty finished trimming and larding a joint of lamb and began to work a spit through it.

"Your friends," she said of Presto, "expect to be through eating before the evening performance. This had better roast in time. Ned, help me lift this."

It was, thought Presto, the least he could do. He went to the hearth, willing to turn the spit for his friends' meal, knowing Betty would not lock him into the wheel forever. She was often enough red-faced herself from the cooking fires. However, he couldn't find the machine and wondered why he hadn't noticed it before. The inn's usual meal was a hearty and ever-changing stew. Perhaps, he thought, the turnspit wheel would have to be set up specially.

"Out of my way now." Ned hefted the spit into place. Presto stood ready to help, but Ned busied himself winding a clocklike mechanism to one side. Then he engaged a chain from it to the end of the spit and adjusted its hanging weights. The machine began to click as the weights pulled down, and the spit turned with no hand or dog near it.

Betty noticed Presto's attention. "Why, you poor little turnspit. You don't have to do this."

*

Later, at the dinner party, O'Connor himself broke his accustomed reticence to raise a glass of port and propose a toast. "To Presto," he said. "Thank Heaven for his safe return."

Dick beamed on the dog, and all the humans repeated, "To Presto." The subject of their attention grinned and looked around embarrassedly.

"What an adventure he must have had," said Mrs. O'Connor. "If only he could tell us about it."

The dogs, who had been told, exchanged glances. "I've heard rumors about that warehouse you were in," said Trig.

Presto felt cold suddenly. "The Spotted Dog?"

"I don't know about him. But a beagle told me the human who owned the place sold it. The new man cleared out a number of dogs."

Presto swallowed.

"He didn't know where they went, but you had best still be careful."

At the table, meanwhile, Mrs. O'Connor completed a humorous monologue, and Dick was prevailed upon for a comic song. After Wilcox and Jonet sang a ballad in parts, Mrs. O'Connor reminded them of the curtain time. They moved out into the taproom, Presto behind Dick, who was laughing at one of O'Connor's jokes, straight into the path of Sligh.

"A merry little party?" he said, more comment than question. Presto's hackles rose. "I have something for you, *Mr.* Oakes." He slapped a document into Dick's hand. Dick stared at it. "If you open it, you will see I am to collect Cruft's puppets. *My* puppets, I should say."

Dick unfolded the paper and read it. The usual noises of talking, laughing, and eating in the room never stopped or slowed.

"Well—" Dick began. Presto growled. "It *looks* legal," Dick continued. "I would like to show this . . ."

"I don't want to make trouble for you," said Sligh quickly. "But if you insist on delaying . . ."

Dick seemed to catch something in the man's voice the same time Presto did. "Trig," yapped Presto. Back in the parlor his friend turned and saw Sligh. He nudged O'Connor's leg to get his attention while Flora slipped out to find Bouncer.

"Let me read this again," Dick said. Presto could see Sligh's eyes shift around the room as if he couldn't wait to leave it. His expression did not improve when O'Connor joined them.

Dick handed the paper to his friend. "What do you know about these things?"

Sligh licked his lips with a flickering motion. "You can't get out of this, you know. Or do you like the thought of debtors' prison?"

"There's something familiar about this," said O'Connor, "only I can't put my finger on it."

"But," Dick said, "I never incurred a debt with you."

"Stole, then. You as good as stole the gear from me." People at the nearer tables began to take notice. This didn't help preserve Sligh's tattering composure, and he was so occupied

100

with his argument that he hadn't yet realized he was encircled by the College of Canines.

Across the room, Presto saw Margery say something to Mrs. Lightfoot. Bouncer returned with Flora and joined the quiet circle of dogs.

"She's coming?" asked Presto.

Bouncer looked worried. "No. Something else is up."

There was a consternation by the door, and everyone, including Sligh, turned to look. Mrs. Lightfoot held a squirming little man by the collar, pulling him up on tiptoe, questioning him. Sligh turned green and tried to slip away. Taffy, the corgi, nipped his ankle to bring him back, yelping, into the circle of dogs, which he noticed for the first time.

"Well, now," said Dick.

"Sligh!" the man in Mrs. Lightfoot's grasp shouted. "You tell her . . ."

"You know each other?" asked O'Connor. "Now I remember."

Margery appeared by Dick's elbow. "That's Scribble the forger. Mrs. Lightfoot's warned him about coming here."

"A forger?" Dick seemed overjoyed at the news and rattled the document in Sligh's face. "What a coincidence."

By now the whole room was watching intently, and a few cheered when Mrs. Lightfoot frog-marched Scribble across the floor to confront Sligh. The dogs silently opened their ranks to admit him.

"You idiot." Sligh had gone from pale to livid.

"I just wanted to see . . ."

"Clotpole!"

"I never get to see it happen. I do all the work and then never see . . ."

Mrs. Lightfoot raised her hand, and they went silent. Scribble cringed, but she only reached for the paper Dick offered. "This is it?" She read it. "Not much of a job. No wonder you aren't successful."

Scribble started to whine, but Sligh belabored him with his hat and the whole room roared. Mrs. Lightfoot jerked her head toward the door, and the two culprits legged it into the dark, straight into the waiting arms of the constable.

Dick drew a deep breath of relief.

"Huh," said Margery. "That's what he gets for hiring cheap help."

*

With renewed confidence, Dick went farther afield with his show, trying it out in the fish markets by the docks, at the vegetable stalls of Covent Garden, at the edges of busy public squares. The problem with crowded places was that too much went on at once; the frequent traffic jams at Charing Cross did not help anyone's temper as the draft horses stamped and snorted, and the chair carriers shouted abuse.

Choice spots were often occupied by other performers, and some of them became outright threatening if Dick looked as though he might offer competition. A pretty young girl singing in one street uttered terrible curses between stanzas, and a strongman act in a courtyard made it clear they were also adept at breaking bones.

Yet Dick and Presto's audiences grew, and they made enough friends among street performers to keep their confidence in the profession. Presto surveyed London from the puppet stage as the winter passed and the city began to turn green in unexpected corners even under the grime of the ever-present coal soot.

He heard the flower-sellers' cries as women came in from the country, hawking elder buds and nettle shoots for spring tonics. He felt the mild spring sun in the open marketplaces and noticed different birds in the parks and squares.

Even the thick fog that came up the Thames and mixed with the city's coal smoke smelled different. When they performed by the water stairs, where little boats would ferry customers across the river, he could see from his perch the bright coats of the watermen appearing and disappearing with their crafts in the fog.

*

One day a man hired them to perform in the street outside his house. A half-dozen children swathed in flannels, confined to the house during some illness, pressed their faces against the window glass in an upstairs room, entranced by the antics of Punch and Presto.

Word seemed to have gotten around, because they were soon hired for a children's party in the home of a linen draper. It was the sort of town house, Presto remembered, the officious spaniel and her puppies had lived in. This time they did the show right in the parlor, to the audience's great delight.

*

Mrs. Lightfoot attempted to find a home for Nimrod with her daughter. But Mrs. Branghton, enthroned at a tea table upstairs from her husband's chandler's shop, thought differently. She already had a fluffy snip of a kitten, Nimrod reported to the other animals, and didn't want a great beast about the place.

"'Beast,' she said," said Nimrod, unsheathing his claws. "That great cow was more interested in reading thrillers like *The Castle of Otranto* — she claimed it gave her nightmares — than in seeing to her poor mouse of a daughter. So I'm to stay here, Mrs. Lightfoot said. Which is fine by me."

*

Dick took Margery to a performance of the O'Connors' troupe. Presto stationed himself in the wings, where he could see both the stage and, with some peering between curtains, the audience. His dog friends leaped and tumbled and chased around each other and the humans. There were also juggling and balancing acts by both species, and a few comic turns by the humans alone, between the more strenuous numbers.

Margery was delighted. Presto saw her initial surprise break into a laughter that continued through every routine. She applauded harder than anyone else when the curtain fell and seemed blissfully astonished by it all when Dick took her backstage to meet his friends.

It was then, while she shook paws with the dogs and patted the pig, that Presto realized he had never heard her laugh before. Perhaps once, he had heard her make a happy sound from another room, but even of that he was uncertain. The gang of children who had pursued her often jeered and snickered, but those were joyless sounds, and Margery, for the most part, remained silent.

But now she was laughing, and, in a surge of joyous sentiment, Presto rubbed his head against her hand.

"I haven't forgotten you," she said, and hugged him tight.

*

Later, back at the Punch Bowl, Margery related the evening's events to Ned and Betty. Dick and Mrs. Lightfoot watched from across the kitchen, and Presto scented their apprehension.

Dick cleared his throat. "Margery." The girl looked his way, still smiling. "Have you ever thought of a theatrical career for yourself? I mean, when you came here it was assumed someone might take you on in one craft or another."

Margery looked alarmed and glanced at Presto.

Dick noticed, and added, "I'm afraid *I* can't. The business . . ."

"It isn't that," said Margery.

Mrs. Lightfoot took charge. "You have to do something, my girl. We thought you might find performing more to your taste."

"But I like it here," she whispered, and Presto's heart wrung in sympathy.

"Domestic service?" said Betty. "You wouldn't find that too dull? We mean something you would stick with."

Margery braided and unbraided her fingers. "No. I mean . . . a little. I mean . . . Mrs. Lightfoot, you taught me numbers and sums. You know what street entertainers make for a living. I don't mean to offend you, Dick Oakes, but you must love puppeteering very much to go through all the trouble of it. There's much more profit in innkeeping. People have to eat, don't they?"

Even Mrs. Lightfoot looked surprised. "Indeed."

105

"But if that's getting above my place . . ." She twisted her apron hem in embarrassment.

Mrs. Lightfoot smiled briefly. Only Presto saw this, as everyone else was staring at the girl. "Very well, Margery. We'll see how you work out," she said.

At first Margery was confused, then she was relieved and joyous all at once. Out loud she said, "I'll do my best, Mrs. Lightfoot."

As Dick and Presto retired up the stairs, they heard the girl asking, "And will you teach me to keep the account books?"

"Law, child. You haven't done multiplication yet."

"Yes, but will you?"

CHAPTER XIII

Wherein doom follows Presto.

A spring rain dampened London for the better part of the week, so it was difficult to find sheltered spots for the puppet show. Dick had to seek out porticoes and colonnades big enough for onlookers. Sometimes these spots were occupied, and sometimes the performers were ordered to move along, so business fell off. After the fourth straight day of this, Presto and Dick sogged back to the inn just as Margery burst into the kitchen. The fragments of cap and apron fluttered after her like cobwebs. There was a cut on one cheek under the mud, and she was laughing.

"I *beat* 'em," she said. "Major wasn't half surprised when I bloodied his snitch."

*

There was a soft rain that night, and the following day fairly quivered with spring, even in the back alleys.

"This is a park sort of day," said Wilcox. "I suggest Saint James's Park. Care to join me?"

That was a new and distant territory for Dick and Presto, but Wilcox had most of London memorized, so the four of them set out, with Bob leading the way on his leash.

St. James's Park proved to be green-scented lawns entwined with paths crowded by humans of all sorts, each astonished to see the sun. Equally astonished cows grazed by a marshy pond dotted with gossiping ducks. In the distance, as Bob indicated, was St. James's Palace, the King's official residence, and Buckingham House to the west, where the Royal Family usually stayed. They also owned the park, but everyone used it.

Presto would have liked to explore the distant canals — there were some deer beyond them among the cattle — but business came first. Women moved among the crowds selling lavender and violets fresh from the country, and a muffin man was somewhere upwind with another, just audible, balladeer.

As it wouldn't do to impinge on another's territory, Dick chose a likely spot near the parade ground, where a crowd had already gathered to watch soldiers drilling. Wilcox unfurled his sheaf of ballads and began singing a humorous number while Dick set up the booth. It was a tribute to Bob's devotion that the dog refrained from howling.

Presto gritted his teeth and gazed at the passing Londoners: well dressed or ragged, proper or of dubious repute — any of them might enjoy a puppet play. He heard a drum roll from over the crowd's heads.

"A flogging," said a passerby. Dick came out of the completed booth and stared toward the troops. Between the onlookers' legs Presto glimpsed a soldier, stripped to the waist, being marched out for public punishment.

Wilcox stopped singing. "We may as well relax until it's over, if it's a flogging. That's a bit of free entertainment the crowds never pass up." He leaned against a tree and took out his pipe. Bob sprawled at his feet on the cool grass, but Presto could see that Dick was anxious.

"One of my brothers joined the army," he said.

They heard the sharp slap of leather on flesh, and then a woman screamed. The babble of the crowd rose as she continued to cry and call out.

"What's that? What's that?" Wilcox demanded. Bob scrambled to his feet.

"A woman," said Dick, craning for a view. "I think she's trying to reach the soldier being beaten."

But others were holding her back, and the flogging continued. Some voices jeered her, then the back of the crowd opened to let her out, and Presto saw her stumble forward, hands to face, being supported and comforted by a middle-aged man in black.

When the sounds of whipping ceased, some burly loafers turned their attention to the woman and, for lack of other entertainment, began making rude remarks about her. Her companion raised his voice, which proved quite carrying, and announced his opinion of people who would rather enjoy the spectacle of their brothers' suffering than extend mercy, of people who knew when to repent and others who had nothing better to do than bully the defenseless.

"Now that would be a Methodist parson," said Wilcox.

"I believe so," said Dick. He eyed the crowd nervously. Presto didn't like the feeling they gave off, and growled.

Someone yelled agreement with the minister, only to be shouted down by his opponents. The better-dressed onlookers hurried off, leaving the rowdier element to their dispute. The woman had stopped crying but looked frightened. Just as the minister started to say something about Christians coming to a peaceable agreement, he was hit in the face by an overripe egg.

Instantly, three or four fights broke out, and the crowd surged toward the puppet booth. Presto yelped, and the woman screamed as the minister fell down. A pair of bruisers lurched between Dick and Wilcox, intent on rearranging each other's face. Dick tried to shout but got an elbow in his stomach. Wilcox staggered, lost his stick, and was pushed farther into the crowd.

Bob barked frenziedly, but before he could go to his human's aid an oversized sailor reeking of gin picked him up by a hind leg and hurled him over several heads towards the struggling minister.

With action quicker than thought, Presto sank his teeth into the sailor's calf, then leaped away to find Bob. He heard his friend yelping, but kicking feet were all about and a straight course was impossible. He saw the woman, no longer weeping, standing by her friend, pulling, despite his exhortations to mercy, at another woman's hair.

Hoofbeats resounded out of the ground, and soon the crowd dissolved into people running away in all directions. Mounted Guards from the nearby barracks had come to stop the melee, and hurrying feet trampled past Presto, bruising his sides and confusing his sense of direction. He was obliged to run before them for a space, and just when he had a chance to turn and look again for Bob, he felt a nip on his haunch.

It was the Spotted Dog himself.

Presto went cold and nearly fell from fright, but the Spotted Dog on one side and Lurcher on the other forced him to run, obscured by the crowd from his friends' sight. They passed beyond a screen of ornamental trees and shrubbery. Far away he could hear Dick calling, "Presto! Presto!" But he could neither answer nor turn back.

When they had put a canal and a grove behind them, the Spotted Dog signaled a halt. "You." He snarled. His eyes seemed smaller than ever. "Traitor. Human-lover. Whispering and snuffling against that door and all the time betraying us to those men."

Presto thought frantically. "In the warehouse, you mean?"

The Spotted Dog bit his shoulder, and Presto shrieked.

"No back talk, pup," said Lurcher. "Some of our best officers died in that raid."

Presto hadn't known that, but was afraid to answer or defend himself.

And so they began to run again, out of the park and into an area that had recently been country but now had new and half-built houses growing on it.

Keeping to fields and hedgerows, they reached one of the villages to the west of London and cautiously approached the shabbier end of it. The sun slid away, and day birds began going to roost. Some small animal darted away down the hedge where the dogs paused to rest, and they could hear a rattle of cans as dairymaids finished the evening milking nearby.

They stopped behind a livery stable near a tavern. It was evident to their noses that no horses had been there for years. Instead, to Presto's surprise, there was the scent of dogs, of rats, and of an all-pervading fear.

"Now." The Spotted Dog smiled. "You go out where you can be seen."

Presto did. He felt as if something might jump him at any moment. He turned nervously, then took a step and stopped when he heard a thick human voice attempting a song. The singer approached unsteadily, tacking on a random course toward the tavern door. He saw Presto and stopped. He smiled, took off his hat, and stretched out a hand.

"Here, doggy. Nishe doggy."

Presto tried to sidestep. Lurcher growled a threat from the hedge, and inside the stable the animals stirred, questioning. The door to the tavern opened, and when Presto shied from that direction, the drunk, with unexpected agility, threw his hat over Presto's head and grabbed him.

Presto choked and snarled in the sudden, sweaty darkness. He heard other men shouting jovially at the drunkard's luck, and under it all he heard the Spotted Dog's low chuckle of satisfaction.

"You got another one, Husk."

"I did," answered Presto's captor. "An thish li'l doggy's gonna pay me debts. Right, boys?" Presto thrashed blindly and was cuffed in the ribs.

Then he felt himself being taken into a dank building and tied by the neck. He lunged and snapped as soon as he could see. Husk swore, though he was untouched, and kicked him.

After the men left and Presto gave up trying to hurl himself against the rope, he noticed there was one other dog, chained to a post across the room.

"They call me Slash." It seemed a formidable name, as he was not unlike Presto. He gestured with his muzzle toward a wall from behind which issued a high-pitched racket.

"Want your throat slit, whelp?" it said. "Just try to start something. Want your guts spilled?"

Presto was aghast. The threats went on and on, becoming fouler and fouler until his fear became anger at the insults.

"Rats," said Slash. "Our adversaries."

"Ours?" He had suspected this, but hearing it was still a shock.

"Well, you see the pit over there, don't you?"

Presto could make out a square wooden enclosure standing chest-high to a human. Tiers of benches rose around it, and there seemed to be wooden shelves closing off the tops of each corner in the pit.

"What's that in the corner?" asked Presto.

Slash glanced over. "Oh, those keep the rats from escaping — most of the time. They'll climb on each other in pyramids to get out."

"Oh."

"Don't worry. We dogs usually win. Once you get the knack, it's almost mechanical. Get a good bite on 'em, give a quick shake, and their necks snap. Of course, if a dog should fall and lose his guard, they'd be all over him in a blink."

"But *why?*"

"The humans think it's fun to watch. Also, they bet a lot of money on the contests. What can we do against that combination? There's a small admission fee, but five rats count as admission too. The money's in the gambling."

The rats quieted, having made their point, but Presto could still feel their fear and fury. "Are we the only dogs?" he whispered.

"More are brought in for the bouts. We're the only ones here now. There were others, but they died."

Presto turned around nervously and curled tightly on the bare floor.

"The next match is tomorrow night," said Slash. Presto shuddered.

*

All in all, it was a sleepless night. The rats in the next shed kept singing fight songs, so, as long as he was awake, Presto chewed at the rope. When the innkeeper entered with water for the dogs, Presto started from a doze straight to his feet. Another man followed, talking about the fights.

"Greetings, Tussle," Slash called out, and Presto saw the head of a Yorkshire terrier peering from the man's coat pocket. Although the tiny dog's hair was as silky as that of many a parlor pet, he possessed all the quivering anticipation of a fighter. He acknowledged Presto's presence with a sniff and proceeded to talk shop with Slash.

Presto was more interested in the water. To judge from the run-down condition of the place, the landlord wasted a good deal of time in chat, as now. Slash had gulped his share, and

Tussle hopped to the floor to sniff an inspection when the land-lord finally brought water to Presto.

Husk came in, lugging a sack. "Ratsh," he said. The sack agitated and let out a fearful screeching that only the dogs, it seemed, could hear. Presto winced and tugged at the rope — it was fraying nicely.

"In there." The landlord jerked his head toward the other room. Tussle's human stepped forward to take the sack, but Husk, muzzy with last night's stout — or possibly with break-fast ale — misunderstood the gesture and pulled the sack out of his reach.

"Ish mine," he said, and dropped it. Either he had tied it insecurely or the captives had gnawed from within, but as soon as the sack hit the floor, rats exploded in all directions.

Husk yelled, Tussle yelped once and whirled into action, and the rats in the next room began screeching again. Presto gave a mighty pull at the rope, which snapped just as a rat ran between the landlord's feet, closely followed by Tussle. When the man fell, Presto sprinted toward the stable door without a backward glance. A young rat preceded him, also intent on escape.

"What a ratter," one of the men shouted. "Get 'em."

But he was out in the yard, over a ditch, and beyond the hedge. Once out of human sight, the rat turned and braced himself against a stone to stand his ground. Presto, who had been following but not chasing, veered aside, close enough to see astonishment replace fear in its red eyes.

He left the village and tore across two plowed fields and a pasture before he paused. Then, when he rested under a hawthorn hedge, he surprised himself further by catching and

115

eating a careless mouse. Some cows came by at this point, their expressions clearly suggesting he leave. He spent the rest of the day wandering in country that looked less and less like London. Although his one desire was to find Dick, hunger and fear of strangers kept diverting him from the roads to the fields and back again, until he was totally confused.

By late afternoon he felt dizzy from fatigue, and drooped along the side of the road, vaguely aware that the river was off to one side. Just as the thought occurred to him that following the river might take him home, he heard a gruff bark from behind, and then, when he did not halt, the thudding of heavy paws.

Presto turned and saw a mastiff bearing down. He had just enough time to notice a butcher's cart pulled by a dusty horse and driven by a florid man as ill-tempered as his dog. Then the mastiff knocked him over.

Presto yelped and rolled away. He scrambled up to run, was bitten on the leg, and fell again. The butcher only watched. The uneven fight continued up the road. Presto got in a few nips but spent most of his energy trying to escape. He dashed around an obelisk at a crossroads and thought he was free, only to feel the mastiff's teeth again. He screamed and fell into a hedge.

A dark shape shot into the road, barking in imperious fury. "How dare you? How dare you?"

The mastiff snarled a curse as Presto tried to rise. His wounded leg buckled in pain, and he collapsed. The mastiff approached, then stopped short as a stone hit the dirt under his nose, followed by a handful of pebbles against his side. A human voice shouted from the direction the stones had come until the butcher grudgingly called off his dog.

"Are you all right?" asked a dog's voice. Presto felt human arms lifting him from the hedge, and then, since he no longer had to resist, he fainted.

CHAPTER XIV

In which Presto begins an entirely new life.

Presto jerked awake from a nightmare about the Spotted Dog and stubbed his nose. His heart racketed in his ears and he sniffed anxiously, but there were only clean scrubbed scents. He was in a box, and above its high wooden sides he could see the tops of cupboards and lines of early morning light around shuttered windows.

He tensed. Dog claws clicked across the floor and scrabbled outside the box. His hackles rose as a pair of dark paws appeared on the rim, followed by the muzzle of a black and tan spaniel.

"Good morning," she said. "I trust you slept well."

"Oh, I . . ."

"A pity," she interrupted, "but understandable. How is your wound?"

He became aware of a bandage on his left hind leg.

She smiled. "Let me introduce myself. I am Rosette."

He balanced on his hind legs and they touched noses over the edge of the box. He felt grubby in the presence of this well-groomed creature. "I'm Presto. Do you live here?"

"I live in the house, yes," she answered, "but not down here in the servants' hall. Of course, sometimes," she added, dropping back to all fours, "we live in London."

Presto watched her walk across the stone-flagged floor and, as she sat with a sweep of her tail to face him, he remembered. "It was *you* who saved me, wasn't it? And that man?"

"Yes," she said modestly. "That was my human, Mr. Walpole."

Presto gazed at her in open admiration. Then they heard footsteps coming downstairs.

Rosette frowned. "The staff. I'll leave now, but you may trust them."

Presto lost his balance and fell back into the box before he could see where she went. When he looked up, the view was filled with the face and mobcap of the scullery maid come to start the fire. She began to coo and gurgle in the way some humans do. "See, Mrs. Young," she called. "He woke up."

The housekeeper appeared, smiled down on him, then gave an order over her shoulder. A footman, grumbling in a foreign language, grasped Presto by the scruff of his neck and took him outside to a service area for a bath. He almost managed a smile when he delivered the dog, now recognizably white and honey-colored, to Mrs. Young for a change of bandage. She examined his leg and smeared cool salve into the torn flesh, remarking all the while about some people who wouldn't control their great hulking curs that attacked innocent little mites.

Then, having been cautioned not to bite the bandage, he was given a plate of scraps while the staff ate breakfast. He dozed, vaguely aware of the housekeeper repeating, "Poor little mite," and woke later when a bell rang in the passage.

The room was empty. He stretched and heard dishes clatter somewhere and a voice say, "That was Mr. Walpole's bell. You can take this up now, Philippe."

The footman passed the door with a covered tray, and Presto, making a quick decision, followed as silently as he could manage. He slipped out the door while the man negotiated tray and door latches, but instead of entering a dining room, Presto found himself in a covered walk off a courtyard by the house's front door, which was open and occupied by a maid scrubbing the threshold. Fortunately, there was a huge Chinese bowl on a pedestal nearby, and the dog pressed behind it while Philippe went past and in at the front door.

As it seemed best to wait, Presto leaned against the pedestal and looked around. The house rose above him in a collection of wings and angles, each sprouting wooden pinnacles and parapets that caught the morning sun. A flock of sparrows quarreled in the ivy over the gate, which, to judge from the rattle of a passing cart, separated the courtyard from the road. He sniffed and was relieved to note the scent of the Thames.

He peered at the maid again and saw she had worked farther into the front hall and had her back to the door. Presto tensed, then sprang into the house and up the stairs. He paused at the first landing, but the maid continued to hum and scrub. As his eyes adjusted to the dimmer light, he saw the stairs angle away above him in a subdued light that glinted off the little gilt antelopes perched on each newel post.

Rosette barked.

Presto perked his ears and at once saw the door standing ajar on the next landing. He ran up and pushed his head in the crack as Rosette barked again. It was a discreet sound, almost like a cough, and Presto realized the situation immediately.

Rosette stood on a chair at a breakfast table set in a three-sided bay that opened onto the lower branches of some linden trees. Presto could see only half of Mr. Walpole, the upper portion being out the window. He leaned forward with one knee on the chair seat in a manner, Presto had been led to believe, foreign to gentlemen, tossing bread to a swarm of finches. A further clamor indicated the sparrows had come round from the gate.

Rosette's warning cough, however, had been directed toward a squirrel teetering on the left-hand sill, with the sun outlining his pointed ears. Mr. Walpole pulled himself back into the room. He scratched Rosette's ears, and she sniffed to make clear her displeasure but leaned into his hand to acknowledge her forgiveness.

Presto sighed. Rosette startled — the breeze from the river had concealed his downwind scent. "Hello, dog," said Mr. Walpole, and knelt to let the dog sniff his hand. He examined Mrs. Young's bandage, scratched Presto behind the ear for good measure, and stood up. They regarded each other a moment while Rosette smiled fondly upon them both. Mr. Walpole, Presto saw, was an angular, middle-aged man whose eyes were nearly as expressive as a spaniel's — at the moment they were expressing amused sympathy — though, in general, he had the briskness of a terrier about him.

There was a rap on the window. "Ho, in there," said the squirrel.

Rosette barked, but Mr. Walpole laughed and gave the squirrel his bread. Rosette watched with distaste as the creature flickered away down the ivy. "What cheek!"

With the intruder out of the way, the dogs were free to enjoy bread and milk of their own while Mr. Walpole finally got around to his own bread, butter, tea, and newspapers. Still exhausted from his ordeal, Presto fell asleep under the table. He was mildly aware of the morning light filling the room, the moving shadows of the linden leaves on the walls, and the quiet undertone of remarks Mr. Walpole made, half to Rosette, half to himself.

Philippe entered to announce the lost dog was lost again, and registered some confusion when Presto came blinking out from under the table. The dog wondered how long he had slept. Rosette was watching squirrels from a window, and Mr. Walpole was busy at a writing desk in the corner.

"Philippe," he said, "put the new dog in the Prior's Garden for a run." The footman grimaced, tucked Presto under his arm, and took him back downstairs into the sunlight.

The Prior's Garden, it turned out, was outside the servants' hall, separated from the front court by a screen of Gothic arches. Once alone, Presto took a quick turn down the length, sniffing. It was safe.

But there was a scrabbling in the courtyard. He whipped around. The sound repeated, and this time he saw Rosette fling herself up the low wall, to wriggle through one of the arches.

She tumbled onto the grass in a most unladylike manner, but sprang up immediately to approach with better dignity.

"Miss Rosette . . ." Presto began.

"Sometimes," she interrupted, "it is necessary *not* to stand on ceremony. Now that you are rested, you must tell me about your adventures. If you don't mind, that is."

"Not at all. I want to tell someone. And the humans don't understand."

"No. The poor dears don't." She settled under a spray of lilac. "Now then, tell your story."

Presto gulped. "I lost my human. I don't know how to begin."

"Ah," said Rosette. "Start at the beginning. Where were you born?"

"Somewhere in London, I suppose. Yes, a livery stable, because I remember the horses going in and out beyond the wall."

"Go on."

"We must have lived in the tack room, because we pups chewed some harness once and the hostler beat us. My mother was warm and kind. She tried to defend us when the men were angry."

"Ah."

"Well, then I was taken away as soon as I was weaned. I never heard of the others after that. Some men came with the stable owner and one snatched me up. 'He's only a runt,' the owner said, and the other answered, 'Good enough for what we want.' He took me away in the rain. I'd never been outside before, and the falling water terrified me. When I struggled, he cuffed me hard on the side of the head and swore."

Rosette shook her head in sympathy.

"When we got to the place where he worked, he took me into the kitchen, where there was an enormous fireplace. I'd never seen fire before either, and I thought they meant to burn me. But though I screamed and kicked out, he shoved me into a wheel-shaped cage."

"A turnspit dog," said Rosette.

"Yes."

"How horrible. I've heard of such practices. We certainly don't allow anything like that in *this* house. But," she continued, "please go on."

And Presto began unburdening himself of his story, as he and Rosette paced the neat walks of the garden under the pinnacles of Strawberry Hill. He described his captivity in detail, and had reached the thrilling escape from the wheel, when Philippe came to retrieve him. Mr. Walpole, on his way to the gate where his carriage waited, wanted to know how Rosette had gotten into the garden, but the footman was unable to invent an answer.

"You make yourself at home, my dear," said Rosette. "I'll be back later." And she trotted off to the carriage while Presto was abruptly carried in to the servants' quarters.

Rosette was, Presto decided, not only beautiful but a good audience. As he dozed in his box, he mentally composed the next installment of his adventures. The wheel and his days and nights alone in London seemed as distant as if they had happened to somebody else.

*

Then began a different era in Presto's life. Some of the

servants at Strawberry Hill were aloof, but no one was unkind. And every day Rosette showed him something new about the place, and listened intently as he told the story of his adventures.

On his second morning, Presto and Rosette explored the area of barn and greenhouse, where there were fascinating heaps of compost and manure to inspect. Mr. Walpole, in the meantime, attempted to get a straight answer from the gardener when he asked that the potted orange trees be taken from the greenhouse to the terrace.

"That's for Mrs. Clive," said Rosette. "She and her brother, Raftor, are coming to tea this afternoon."

"Catherine Clive? O'Connor mentioned her. He admired her comedy."

"Oh, yes. *The* Clive. They live across the field, over there." Rosette frowned and circled the gardener where he leaned against a wheelbarrow.

"Oh no," he was saying to Mr. Walpole, "that won't do at all."

"And why not, Cowie?" If Mr. Walpole had been a dog, his hackles would have bristled. As it was, he could only put an edge to his voice.

"The weather. Never can be sure of the weather for them trees."

Rosette coughed meaningfully. "What that man needs is a good nip on the ankle. He just doesn't want the work of putting the trees back afterward."

The dogs left the humans arguing the matter and entered the barn. The scents there were as fascinating as those outside. A flock of bantams moved warily in the shadows, but all the other residents were out. Or so they thought until a cat suddenly appeared halfway up the loft ladder.

The dogs started. "It's just Harold, the barn cat," said Rosette, to cover her embarrassment.

"No 'just' about it, house dog. Who's your friend?"

"My friend," said Rosette testily — and the hair was standing on her neck — "is an actor from the London stage. Something *you* wouldn't know about."

The cat uncoiled and strolled along the edge of the loft. "Wouldn't I?" he murmured. "But don't let me stop you. Have your little talk."

Rosette showed her teeth. "You give cheek like that because you know I'm under oath not to bite. I, who am descended from the royal dogs of the second King Charles."

"La-de-da," said Harold rudely. "Fidos-come-lately don't impress me, who am descended" — he mimicked Rosette's tone — "from Cardinal Wolsey's favorite cat."

Rosette elevated her muzzle a few degrees. "Come along, Presto. Let me show you the greenhouse."

They left the cat snickering, and when they were out of sight Presto could see Rosette still had a dangerous gleam in her eye. They worked their way around the greenhouse, stopping to sniff the various cuttings and prunings tossed out, and the ashes from the furnace.

"It wouldn't be a bad idea if you stayed on here," said Rosette. "As you just saw, the cats need keeping in their place."

Presto continued his story, introducing with dramatic flair the perils of street life and the Spotted Dog. They strolled in the formal gardens while he talked, and sat on the curb of a pool to watch the goldfish. He concluded with his finding Dick, and paused. Rosette sat in thoughtful silence, her long curling ears hanging forward on either side of her dark moist nose.

Presto felt almost heady from the fresh country scents and the variety of birdsong, both so different from the smells and noise of London. Rosette had begun to speak, when she was interrupted by a rude baa-ing from behind. One of the ornamental goats crashed through the hedge and stood staring from under a fragment of honeysuckle twined around three of her four horns, drooping rakishly over her demented yellow eyes. She grinned around a mouthful of syringa. "What ho, dogs."

"Our flowers!" Rosette exclaimed. "You get back where you belong."

It took much barking, dodging, and herding around the pool, out the hedge, and into the barnyard, but once there, the gardener's boy took over and prodded the unrepentant goat, still giggling, to her proper pasture.

Presto and Rosette trotted back to the house. All in all, it was very satisfying.

*

Mrs. Clive was audible long before she was visible. She arrived, not at the front gate as Presto had expected, but stepping along a path through the meadows, scattering sheep with her hallooing.

"Catherine Clive," said Rosette, "was a great beauty in her youth, and a fine singer."

She still had command of her voice, Presto noticed, but now

127

made two of Mr. Walpole. Her brother, the sort of man easily overlooked, was not left out of the exchange of greetings, but it was evident, as the party moved across the garden, that his share in the conversation would be limited for the most part to nods and smiles.

There were no orange trees to be seen. The tea table was set up in the shelter of the Great Cloister, whose open arches afforded a fine view across the lawn to the grove.

Presto perked his ears. Mr. Walpole was explaining the terrier's presence while the guests regarded the dog sympathetically. He wagged his tail, and Mrs. Clive scratched behind his ear.

While the humans continued their talk, Presto ran about the lawn to work off the emotion raised by this attention. Then, panting, he came to rest on the Cloister's cool flagstones next to Rosette. She licked a bit of icing from her nose. Tea had arrived.

Mr. Walpole did more talking than eating. Mrs. Clive continued to engage in both activities with equal gusto, while Mr. Raftor listened, smiling and nodding, and slipped some cakes to the dogs.

"It's a strange thing," said Presto. "During these months since my escape I've met all kinds of dogs and all kinds of people, and I still don't know what to expect."

"How so?"

"Well, some dogs bit before you had a chance to do anything, but others were just afraid. It was a terrible life, alone in the streets, so it's easy to think that's what makes the dogs nasty. But there were well-cared-for dogs just as mean. Not like you," he added hastily when Rosette twitched an ear. "After all, you saved my life."

"If you think dogs are complicated, try figuring out humans."

"Oh, I know," he agreed. "The Otways put me in their terrible wheel, but they let Fuzz do anything. Well-dressed men have kicked me without a second thought, and then Dick" — he swallowed hard — "shared his last crust with me. Later, some poor men were after me for the pits, but Mr. Walpole has been the soul of kindness."

"You're becoming a philosopher."

"At least we dogs can scent out moods. These humans have no skill with their noses. I don't know how they get on at all."

"I expect some other sense is sharper to make up for the lack." Rosette paused to consider this and frowned. "I have met a number of irritating dogs in my time, sir, but far more unbearable people. And you notice they use the terms 'manly' and 'humane' as compliments." She snorted, and the two of them had to run up and down the lawn several times to settle themselves.

Then, as Mrs. Clive and her brother were about to leave, Presto heard the distant chime of a bell at the front gate. After a moment the housekeeper appeared.

"Mr. Walpole," she said. "There is a party wishing to see the house."

His face fell, and Mrs. Clive said, "More of them?"

"Like invading troops," said Mr. Walpole.

"They seem well behaved," Mrs. Young added.

"Oh — yes. Very well. But you show them around. I'll have to hope they don't see with their fingers."

Mrs. Clive said something about gawping sightseers, and soon voices drifted from the house as the tour began. *"Such* a famous house — heard absolutely *marvelous* things about it. Now can you tell us about that piece . . . ?"

Mr. Walpole winced and offered to walk his guests across the meadow.

CHAPTER XV
Wherein a Gothic mystery is encountered.

Sometimes it actually rained at Strawberry Hill. Presto was used to getting wet if that happened to be the weather — which it often was — but now he felt it comfortable indeed to sit with Rosette on a windowseat in the Long Gallery and watch the spring rain soak into the lawn. Cool green scents twined damply and deliciously through the window to the dogs' noses, until a passing footman reached between them and shut it firmly.

"Very well," said Rosette. "Mr. Walpole doesn't like drafts."

Presto had noticed his host's joints stiffened in damp weather. Just now, Mr. Walpole was close to the fire in the Library, sorting new additions to his print collection.

"We will be going back to London soon." said Rosette. "Mr.

Walpole must get back for Parliament. I wish he wouldn't spend so much time at that. It gets him all worked up."

"I wonder if it's anything like the meeting of dogs I was taken to," said Presto.

"I hope not," said Rosette. "Some of the members are rowdy, but mainly it's all talk and no teeth. Not like wars, now."

Presto turned around and sat down again. "That's another thing. One of Dick's brothers is a soldier and I've seen soldiers drilling, but what do they do?"

"I've never seen a war, either," said Rosette. "I gather that it's like a brawl, only bigger and with guns, and it goes on and on. For *years*, sometimes."

Presto flicked his ears in amazement. He wasn't sure he believed that. "The Spotted Dog was the fiercest dog I've ever met," he said, "but I don't think even he could keep up a fight for years. Begging your pardon, Miss Rosette, but it just doesn't seem possible."

"Well, they do," she snapped. "I never said they were sensible."

He thought more about this and still couldn't make head or tail of it. So he recounted the next stage of his adventures to Rosette, describing all the horrors of his capture and escape from the Spotted Dog and his pack.

Rosette did not conceal her admiration, but by then it was evening and they both felt the need for human companionship. There were too many shadows in the Gallery, and the portraits that lined the walls and reflected out of the mirrors seemed too much like a silent, staring crowd. So they went down the corridors to join Mr. Walpole in his Library. Rosette greeted her human where he sat writing at a desk, and then reclined by Presto on the hearth.

Bookcases lined the room behind carved arches that in the flickering firelight seemed to sway slightly, like plants in a breeze.

"Your Mr. Walpole," said Presto, "seems to like that archy, spidery stuff. It's all over the house."

"Gothic," said Rosette. "Yes, it amuses him. I gather it is the sort of design humans used to make a long time ago — at least on churches and things. These walls are patterned after a tomb somewhere."

"Oh? How odd." The only sounds were the crackling fire and the scratching of Mr. Walpole's quill. The effect was quite peaceful.

Rosette shifted position. "Since he started this, Gothic has become all the vogue. He wrote a novel with a Gothic setting a while ago — knights, castles, ghosts, and all."

This sounded familiar. "Not *The Castle of Otranto?*"

"Why, yes." She seemed surprised.

"Nimrod told me. Mrs. Branghton was reading it and scaring herself silly. Now I remember."

Rosette smiled. "I hear it's still going over well. What most humans don't realize is that the castle in the book is patterned after Strawberry Hill. Not exactly, of course. The castle is a vast place. I mean the rooms connect the same way. That's something writers do, I gather. They take a few facts and toy around with them."

"And then," Presto said, "I suppose some readers think the whole thing is fact."

"Visitors will be wanting to be shown the secret tunnel next."

"Oh — is there one?"

"Of course not." Rosette seemed annoyed at his mistake and turned to scratch behind an ear with one hind foot.

Embarrassed, Presto tried to make a joke of it. "No ghost either, I presume."

But Rosette hesitated, paw in air, then composed herself and turned back to Presto. He saw a gleam of excitement in her eyes. "To tell you the truth, there is."

Presto startled.

"The humans don't know it, not even Mr. Walpole."

"It must be a very quiet ghost."

"Yes, well, it's a cat, you see. And she isn't always there. Do you remember the big Chinese bowl near the front entrance?"

Presto nodded.

"Well, it used to be full of water and have goldfish in it. Long before my time a cat who lived here fell in and drowned while trying to catch the fish."

"Poor cat."

Rosette sniffed. "Silly creature ought to have known better than climb on a slippery thing like that. At any rate, we animals sometimes see her ghost."

"Now *that* would be something."

"Oh? Well, I think we might arrange it."

"You can?" Presto wondered if he really wanted her to, but Rosette seemed enormously pleased with the idea and jumped up with a yip of excitement that startled Mr. Walpole out of his revery. By way of apology, Rosette retrieved his quill from where it had rolled under the desk, then flung herself down by Presto.

"Of course, I can't promise we will see anything, but I think this will be interesting all the same."

*

Rosette's plans proved more elaborate than Presto had suspected. On the next day she went off to the barn to confer with Harold, who, being a cat, was reputed to possess mystical powers.

In addition, Mr. Walpole, all unaware of the plan afoot, had invited some of his politically minded friends for an evening of cards and conversation.

"That ought to keep everyone busy," said Rosette as the guests began arriving. Then, as an apprehensive pug entered, she called out, "Oh, hello there, Raton. Let me introduce you to a new friend."

The pug approached with the weight of the world on his shoulders, and rolled an eye at Presto as if he were afraid the terrier might bite. Rosette gave a summary of Presto's adventures, which seemed to impress the pug. They exchanged sniffs under their hostess's approving gaze and wagged a welcome to each other.

"Raton," she continued, "is an old and dear friend. That Mr. Selwyn over there is his human." She gestured toward a sleepy-looking individual handing his hat to a footman. "A great wit," she added.

The dogs milled around the edges, taking care to avoid the ladies' swirling petticoats, as the humans' talk began with commonplaces about the weather, proceeded to more specific subjects, and, sparked by an occasional *bon mot,* took off at a good clip when someone mentioned the working conditions of chimney sweeps. By the time it was fully dark, and Rosette decided they ought to leave, Mr. Walpole was becoming very hot on the subject of certain rebels in the American colonies with whose cause he agreed. Fortunately, so did most of those assembled.

The dogs slipped out the front door to the little court between house and gate. To their left the Chinese bowl gleamed coolly in the moonlight.

Suddenly, a cat appeared before them on the flagstones. Raton shuddered visibly enough to obscure the fact that Rosette had also flinched.

"Hello, Harold," said Rosette with the slightest edge to her voice. "You know everyone already, don't you?"

"Good Lord," said Raton, "but you gave us a start."

Harold smiled. Despite the dimness, Presto saw that he was actually quite an old cat. His motions, though stiff, were full of dignity. "Good evening, my children," he said. Rosette sniffed, but he ignored her. "Perhaps, as requested, I may be able to contact the Lady Selima — this is the season wherein she walks — but I must have complete cooperation and *no* interruptions."

"What if . . ." Raton began nervously.

"*No* interruptions," said Harold. He stalked toward the Little Cloister with his tail as straight as a flagpole. He stepped up to its level and turned to the dogs. "Sit in a semicircle behind me, facing the bowl."

They did, with some nervous snuffling from Raton, who had to turn around three times first and even then shifted from haunch to haunch until Harold glared at him. Presto poised for sudden action. He glanced at Rosette and saw that, although she sat in a composed manner, she nevertheless had a certain tightness about her muzzle whenever the cat gave an order.

Just as Harold began a low chant, Presto noticed a gleam of light over Rosette's head by the gate. He turned and gasped. The whole wall between the court and the road was alight with the reflecting eyes of cats.

"Hush!" Harold commanded.

Rosette yipped once in indignation. "What is the meaning of this?"

"Be quiet," the cat snapped. "I admit I let word get around. This is meaningful for cats, you know."

Rosette didn't deign to reply.

Harold began to chant again, low at first, then rising and falling in pitch. Presto could understand none of it and assumed the incantation was in pure feline. Yet — and he glanced at Rosette's skeptical expression — he could not be sure that the cat wasn't making some of it up, just to impress them. He felt the hackles rise as the chant went on. Raton rolled his eyes and shuddered.

The cats on the wall joined in on the responses, then stopped, so suddenly that the silence seemed a new sound.

There was a slight disturbance in the air above the bowl. Harold gave a command, and it grew brighter. The cats on the wall vibrated silently. Rosette gasped, and Presto had to shoulder against Raton to keep him upright.

Slowly, a dim form rose from the depths of the Chinese bowl, hovered above it, and materialized on its lofty side as a calico cat.

"The Lady Selima!" Harold intoned.

She was soaked to the skin and had her ears flat back in fury as she teetered on the brim, glaring at the spectators.

"What is all this," said the ghost of Selima. *"Who do you think you are, staring at me?"*

All the cats on the wall gave a screech, and Raton fell over. Presto never saw what Selima did next. The house door flew open. A footman ran out to see what had happened. Mr. Walpole arrived just as the cats' eyes blinked, then the wall exploded ivy leaves. Everyone heard the thudding of cats landing on the dirt of the road outside.

The dogs wasted no time streaking indoors and rounding the stairs into one of the unoccupied rooms. They flung themselves on the carpet and tried to look as if they had been there for hours.

Mrs. Young regarded them from the door. Rosette smiled winningly. The housekeeper said nothing to them but turned to one of the maids behind her.

"Something has dripped water in the Little Cloister. See that it's mopped up before the guests leave."

CHAPTER XVI

Wherein Presto decides his own fate.

Next afternoon, Mr. Walpole played a game of catch with Presto and Rosette before leaving to supervise the planting of some exotic shrubs. The dogs chose to explore the walks in the grove while Presto concluded the story of his adventures.

Now that his leg was well again and several idyllic days were between him and the narrow escapes he described, the action seemed remote, and he exaggerated slightly, in a melodramatic manner.

Rosette was attentive as always, her interest evident even when she veered off to chase a squirrel or examine an unusual scent. She expressed horror at his kidnapping, indignation at the rat pit, and elation at his escape. Yet there was a certain reserve in her manner, which, when he noticed it, made him dramatize the more.

"And so I lay, nearly expiring, under the hedge, once more struck down by cruel fate and knowing no more until I awoke and saw you." Presto cast a languishing eye toward his audience.

"And here you are," Rosette said wryly. "What adventures will you have next? Or do you plan a quieter life for yourself?"

They came out of the trees to a knoll, where a bench shaped like a shell overlooked a stream. Rosette hopped onto the bench and faced him. "You could live here," she went on. "I'm sure Mr. Walpole would be agreeable. The cats do tend to overstep themselves while I'm in London."

Presto hadn't thought of that possibility. So far, events had simply carried him on, but once the question had been put to him directly, he knew at once his answer.

"I must go back and find Dick."

"It's a long way. And you know how many dangers there are."

"It doesn't matter. I have to do it."

She smiled. "London is downstream."

"I must go now. I can travel all night. Good-by, Miss Rosette. Please give my repects to Mr. Walpole."

He leaped the stream and ran down the slope to the Thames.

"Farewell," Rosette called.

Birds flew up before him; rabbits darted to either side. He took bearings from the river and began the journey back.

*

Presto passed through the village of Twickenham with leaps and bounds, then settled into a brisk walk he could keep up for hours. It was necessary to veer away from the river now and again when large dogs on barges barked low warnings. Dogs on the road and in yards seemed best avoided as well, yet all the time, he was aware of the river off to the right and kept checking for its scent among the crowding scents of evening.

He rested a while in a cow pasture, unsure if he had dreamed or seen tiny lights moving in the grass. A hedgehog blundered by and squeaked, "May Eve," in answer to Presto's question. He did not understand, yet he felt the excitement in the hedgerows and noticed that even the cows, silhouetted on the field's far edge, were gazing at the stars.

There was music in the woods he passed from either reed pipes or the wind. The night was full of life and hope. There was no room for despair. Though the way be blocked by rats or traps, he thought, rogue humans or whole packs of Spotted Dogs, yet he would find his friends.

He was in the outskirts of London by dawn. Carts and barges were moving out of the mist toward the day's markets. Something else was stirring in the villages that ringed the city. Presto heard music and the rhythmical shaking of bells. He kept on along the river until its reedy banks became built up with wharves and promenades, warehouses and water stairs. He began recognizing places now, and swerved into the streets and alleys, rejoicing in their familiarity.

Presto dashed through a court to take a short cut and came out into the middle of a noisy procession. Even in the gray heart of London the humans were bringing in summer with ceremonies so old they no longer understood them, so ancient that only the Tower ravens knew their meaning.

A band of chimney sweeps surrounded him, to block his way

and make him join the dance. As they jigged, little puffs of flour drifted from their heads, for they had powdered over their soot-stained skins and donned the cast-off wigs of gentlemen. Behind them danced the milk women, who, once he eluded the boys, danced around him also, shaking their petticoats in his face. One caught him from behind and thrust a nosegay under his collar.

All the women carried flowers or helped push an enormous, clattering construction in a cart. It appeared to be a pyramid of silver urns and plates and teapots stuck all over with flowers, and flashing back the sun in blinding rays. Some women balanced smaller pyramids on their heads as they danced.

Presto reeled in confusion. A Fool shook bells under his nose, a Hobbyhorse snapped its wooden jaws, and just when he thought he was free, he came up against the Green Man. It was a man in a wickerwork frame covered in leaves, their bruised stems still pungent with sap. Yet there was something old and wild about this figure of summer, something more than a little threatening.

Presto turned a near somersault and doubled back, to the crowd's applause, and escaped into the street. He heard laughter behind him, then a familiar squeaky voice ahead that was cut off sharply, drowned out by shouting. Passersby, having watched the procession, now turned their attention to an angry crowd around a puppet booth.

"Me pocket's been picked!" a woman yelled. "Call the Watch."

Now the general muttering turned to accusations as more people noticed they had been robbed. "These showmen team up with pickpockets," someone shouted. "Make him give our money back."

Dick came out of the booth, protesting, right into the barnacle grip of a large and enraged fishwife, who ignored any and all explanations he tried to offer.

Presto yelped frantically, but his way was blocked by the crowd's milling feet. The watchmen arrived just as someone started throwing fish heads at Dick. Presto raced around the mob but could not squeeze through. He stood back, head whirling, and caught a familiar, sour scent. It was Dip, standing only a few yards away, extracting a moneybag from under a man's coattails. His victim was too intent on shouting abuse at Dick to notice.

Quicker than thought, Presto hurtled forward and fastened his teeth in Dip's leg. The pickpocket screeched, shot into the air, and landed shouting. Presto had no intention of letting loose no matter how much he was buffeted.

"Get 'im off, get 'im off, get 'im *off!*"

"Tell the truth," yelled Dick, "and then I might call him off."

The crowd turned to this new commotion.

"Ow, ow, ow, wow. Yes. Yes, I did it. That stupid puppeteer and his vicious dog aren't any part of it. I wouldn't team with him if you promised me the crown jewels."

Presto let go, gagged a little, and staggered out of the way. The watchmen clumped over to take charge, joined by the fishwife, who got ahead of them, grabbed Dip before he could escape, and jammed him in a nearby barrel of fish guts. As it took a while for the watchmen to extract him from this and

143

lead him off to jail, the crowd was well distracted. Presto ran to Dick, who knelt to scoop him up.

"Presto," he said. The dog lapped his chin. "Presto."

*

Dog and man returned in triumph to the Punch Bowl. When she saw them, Mrs. Lightfoot put her hand to her heart and said, "Well!" Presto had seldom seen her so emotional. Margery shrieked and grabbed him before he had time to side-step.

"The prodigal returns," said Nimrod, his sarcasm not quite masking his relief. "And wreathed in flowers, to boot. I suppose the next time he disappears, he will come back in a coach and six."

To Presto's surprise, nearly everyone who knew them was glad to see his return. When he and Dick performed in the streets, regular customers called out greetings and stopped to chat after the show. Presto hardly knew how to contain all his happiness, and was given to frisks and capers. He suspected the Spotted Dog was still at large, and he knew there were crowds of cruel humans and even more who were indifferent. Yet he knew he was loved. He imagined Dick at the center of a circle with all their friends around them from Margery to Mr. Walpole, and beyond them a larger circle of the audiences they had delighted.

"If I should die tomorrow in the pits," he declared to himself — and he shuddered at the idea and the recollection of other dogs who might have to — "I shall know I am loved."

It wouldn't keep off danger, though somehow it seemed

contrast to the offhand cruelties and deliberate tortures directed at other animals, including such practices as cock-fights and dog-fights.

The people of the time left much evidence of themselves in words, pictures, and artifacts. Many of the character types and scenes in *Presto* were suggested by the work of artists William Hogarth and Thomas Rowlandson, who recorded all facets of their times but preferred to satirize the seamier side. Some of the story's characters, however, actually lived. Samuel Johnson, author of essays and the first modern dictionary, did slip coins for breakfast to sleeping street urchins as Hester Thrale, one of his friends and biographers, noted. Everyone at Strawberry Hill is real, including the goats. The many and often humorous letters of Horace Walpole are the best single source of information on his time. Rosette once saved his life when the chimney was on fire and only she knew about it. Granted, the ghost is my invention, but the true watery end of Selima was immortalized by Walpole's friend Thomas Gray in his "Ode on the Death of a Favorite Cat, Drowned in a Tub of Gold Fishes," wherein we learn that:

Not all that tempts your wand'ring eyes
And heedless hearts, is lawful prize;
  Nor all that glisters, gold.

greater than that. But the thoughts were too much for him, so he flipped a backward somersault, the way Trig had taught him.

*

Dick, along with the juggler and the man with the Educated Pig from the O'Connors' show, decided to put together an act and travel among the fairs all summer. They held a modest farewell dinner at the Punch Bowl for their friends.

The O'Connors offered useful advice. "We'll see you in September at Bartholomew Fair," said Trig. "Keep your tail wagging."

Then a fiddler struck up a jig, and the company set to dancing around the table until closing time came and went, and Mrs. Lightfoot persuaded them to jig out the door so that she could close shop.

*

Dick ended his work at the cow house the next morning and returned to the Punch Bowl for his belongings.

"You can depend on a room here at summer's end," said Mrs. Lightfoot. "Presto, too." She leaned down to scratch his ear.

Margery reached in and tied a gift of ribbon round his neck. "I'll wait here for you," she whispered.

Nimrod and Bouncer watched from the side.

"Such a tender scene," said the cat. But when they were ready to leave he called after them, "Watch out for sharpers."

Dick shifted the straps that held his burden, and they set out together through the streets of London, Presto dancing before. He leaped, he jumped, he turned a somersault for joy, until Dick laughed aloud.

"Ho, Presto."

THE END

NOTES

Presto's fictional adventures take place in the London from the Twelve Days after Christmas when the ancien and the Dragon return-to-life folk play was performed, ancient and pagan May Day ceremonies where the cele queraded as the forces of nature personified. (Some of th survive in England today.)

Although the use of a living Toby-Dog with the Punc shows did not become common in England until the n there were elaborate dog acts, such as Madam Midnight' assumed small-time puppeteers like Dick Oakes could tried such an experiment.

Eighteenth-century England held widely differing view treatment of animals. Scientific demonstrations of intel and the lives of well-loved pets like Rosette provide